the GARF

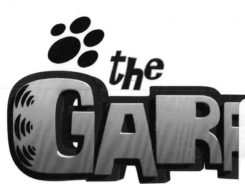

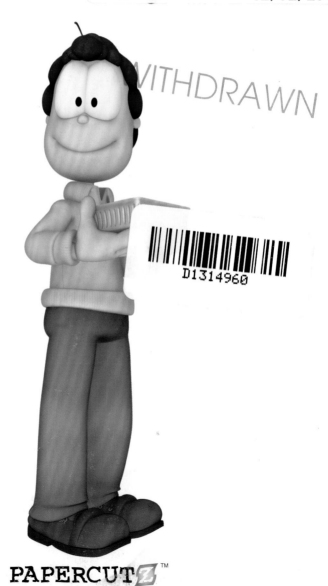

PAPERCUTZ™

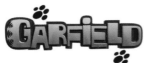

GARFIELD GRAPHIC NOVELS AVAILABLE FROM PAPERCUTZ™

GARFIELD
FISH TO FRY
& Co
PAPERCUTZ

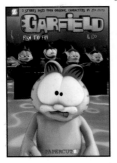

GARFIELD & Co #1
"FISH TO FRY"

GARFIELD
THE CURSE OF THE CAT PEOPLE
& Co
PAPERCUTZ

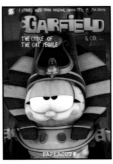

GARFIELD & Co #2
"THE CURSE OF THE CAT PEOPLE"

GARFIELD
"CATZILLA"
& Co
PAPERCUTZ

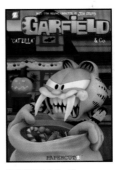

GARFIELD & Co #3
"CATZILLA"

GARFIELD
"CAROLING CAPERS"
& Co
PAPERCUTZ

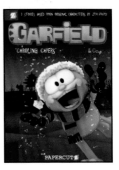

GARFIELD & Co #4
"CAROLING CAPERS"

GARFIELD
A GAME OF CAT AND MOUSE
PAPERCUTZ

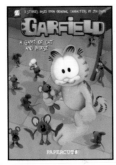

GARFIELD & Co #5
"A GAME OF CAT AND MOUSE"

GARFIELD
MOTHER GARFIELD
PAPERCUTZ

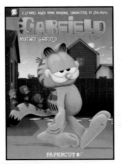

GARFIELD & Co #6
"MOTHER GARFIELD"

GARFIELD
HOME FOR THE HOLIDAYS
PAPERCUTZ

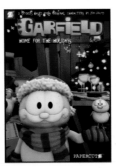

GARFIELD & Co #7
"HOME FOR THE HOLIDAYS"

GARFIELD
SECRET AGENT X

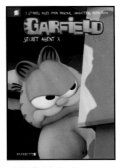

GARFIELD & Co #8
"SECRET AGENT X"

GARFIELD
show
UNFAIR WEATHER
PAPERCUTZ

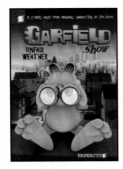

THE GARFIELD SHOW #1
"UNFAIR WEATHER"

the GARFIELD show
JON'S NIGHT OUT
PAPERCUTZ

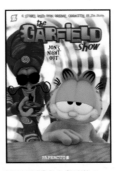

THE GARFIELD SHOW #2
"JON'S NIGHT OUT"

the GARFIELD show
LONG LOST LYMAN
PAPERCUTZ

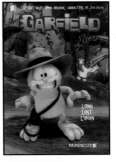

COMING SOON:
THE GARFIELD SHOW #3
"LONG LOST LYMAN"

GARFIELD & Co GRAPHIC NOVELS ARE AVAILABLE IN HARDCOVER ONLY FOR $7.99 EACH.
THE GARFIELD SHOW GRAPHIC NOVELS ARE $7.99 IN PAPERBACK, AND $11.99 IN HARDCOVER.
AVAILABLE FROM BOOKSELLERS EVERYWHERE.

YOU CAN ALSO ORDER ONLINE FROM PAPERCUTZ.COM OR CALL 1-800-886-1223, MONDAY THROUGH FRIDAY, 9 - 5 EST. MC, VISA, AND AMEX ACCEPTED. TO ORDER BY MAIL, PLEASE ADD $4.00 FOR POSTAGE AND HANDLING FOR FIRST BOOK ORDERED, $1.00 FOR EACH ADDITIONAL BOOK, AND MAKE CHECK PAYABLE TO NBM PUBLISHING. SEND TO: PAPERCUTZ, 160 BROADWAY, SUITE 700, EAST WING, NEW YORK, NY 10038.

GARFIELD & Co AND THE GARFIELD SHOW GRAPHIC NOVELS ARE ALSO AVAILABLE WHEREVER E-BOOKS ARE SOLD

the GARFIELD show

#2 "Jon's Night Out"

BASED ON THE ORIGINAL CHARACTERS CREATED BY

JIM DAVIS

PAPERCUTZ ™

NEW YORK

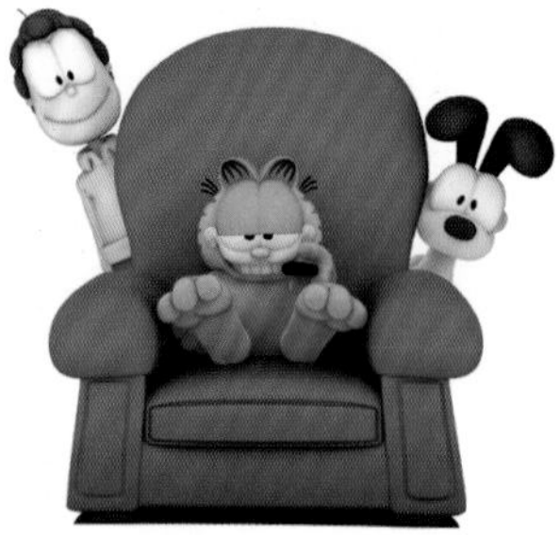

THE GARFIELD SHOW #2 "JON'S NIGHT OUT"

 THE GARFIELD SHOW—A DARGAUD MEDIA PRODUCTION. IN ASSOCIATION WITH FRANCE3 WITH THE PARTICIPATION OF CENTRE NATIONAL DE CINÉMATOGRAPHIE AND THE SUPPORT OF REGION ILE-DE-FRANCE. A SERIES DEVELOPED BY PHILIPPE VIDAL, ROBERT REA AND STEVE BALISSAT. BASED UPON THE CHARACTERS CREATED BY JIM DAVIS. ORIGINAL STORIES: "NIGHT OF THE APPARATUSES" AND "BLASTEROID" WRITTEN BY EMMANUELLE AUBERT WITH DIALOGUE POLISH BY MARK EVANIER; "ME, GARFIELD & I" WRITTEN BY CHRISTOPHE PUJOL; "PASTA WARS" WRITTEN BY MARK EVANIER; "JON'S NIGHT OUT" AND "THE ROBOT" WRITTEN BY BAPTISTE HEIDRICH & JULIEN MONTHIEL; "NIGHT OF THE BUNNY SLIPPERS" WRITTEN BY JULIEN MAGNAT.

CEDRIC MICHIELS - COMICS ADAPTATION
JOE JOHNSON - TRANSLATIONS
JIM SALICRUP - DIALOGUE RESTORATION
MICHAEL PETRANEK - LETTERING
BETH SCORZATO - PRODUCTION COORDINATOR
MICHAEL PETRANEK - ASSOCIATE EDITOR
JIM SALICRUP
EDITOR-IN-CHIEF

ISBN: 978-1-59707-443-8 PAPERBACK EDITION
ISBN: 978-1-59707-444-5 HARDCOVER EDITION

PRINTED IN CHINA
AUGUST 2013 BY O.G. PRINTING PRODUCTIONS, LTD.
UNITS 2 & 3, 5/F, LEMMI CENTRE
50 HOI YUEN ROAD
KWON TONG, KOWLOON

PAPERCUTZ BOOKS MAY BE PURCHASED FOR BUSINESS OR PROMOTIONAL USE. FOR INFORMATION ON BULK PURCHASES PLEASE CONTACT MACMILLAN CORPORATE AND PREMIUM SALES DEPARTMENT AT (800) 221-7945 X5442.

DISTRIBUTED BY MACMILLAN
FIRST PAPERCUTZ PRINTING

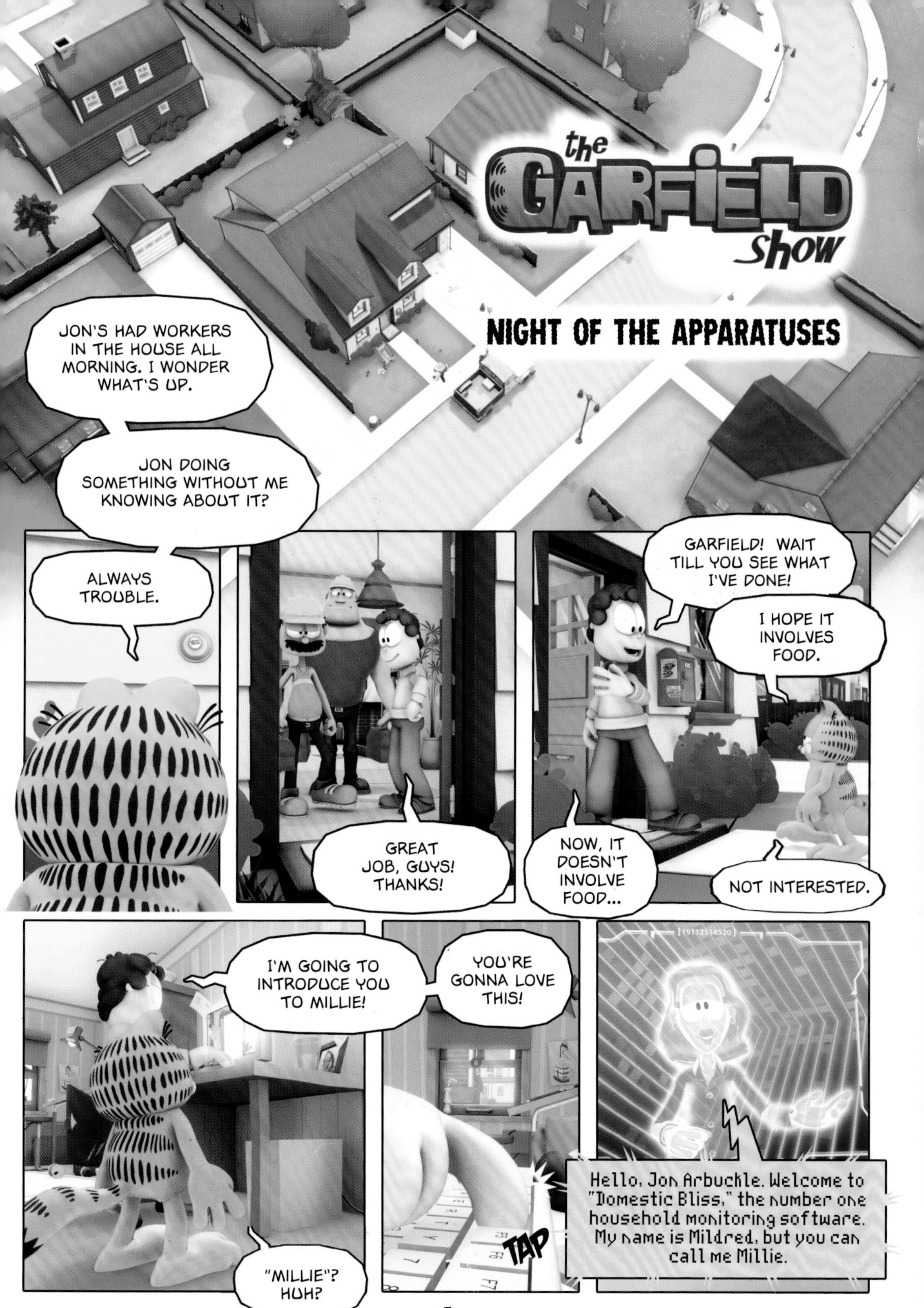
the GARFIELD show
NIGHT OF THE APPARATUSES
JON'S HAD WORKERS IN THE HOUSE ALL MORNING. I WONDER WHAT'S UP.
JON DOING SOMETHING WITHOUT ME KNOWING ABOUT IT?
ALWAYS TROUBLE.
GREAT JOB, GUYS! THANKS!
GARFIELD! WAIT TILL YOU SEE WHAT I'VE DONE!
I HOPE IT INVOLVES FOOD.
NOW, IT DOESN'T INVOLVE FOOD...
NOT INTERESTED.
I'M GOING TO INTRODUCE YOU TO MILLIE!
"MILLIE"? HUH?
YOU'RE GONNA LOVE THIS!
TAP
Hello, Jon Arbuckle. Welcome to "Domestic Bliss," the number one household monitoring software. My name is Mildred, but you can call me Millie.

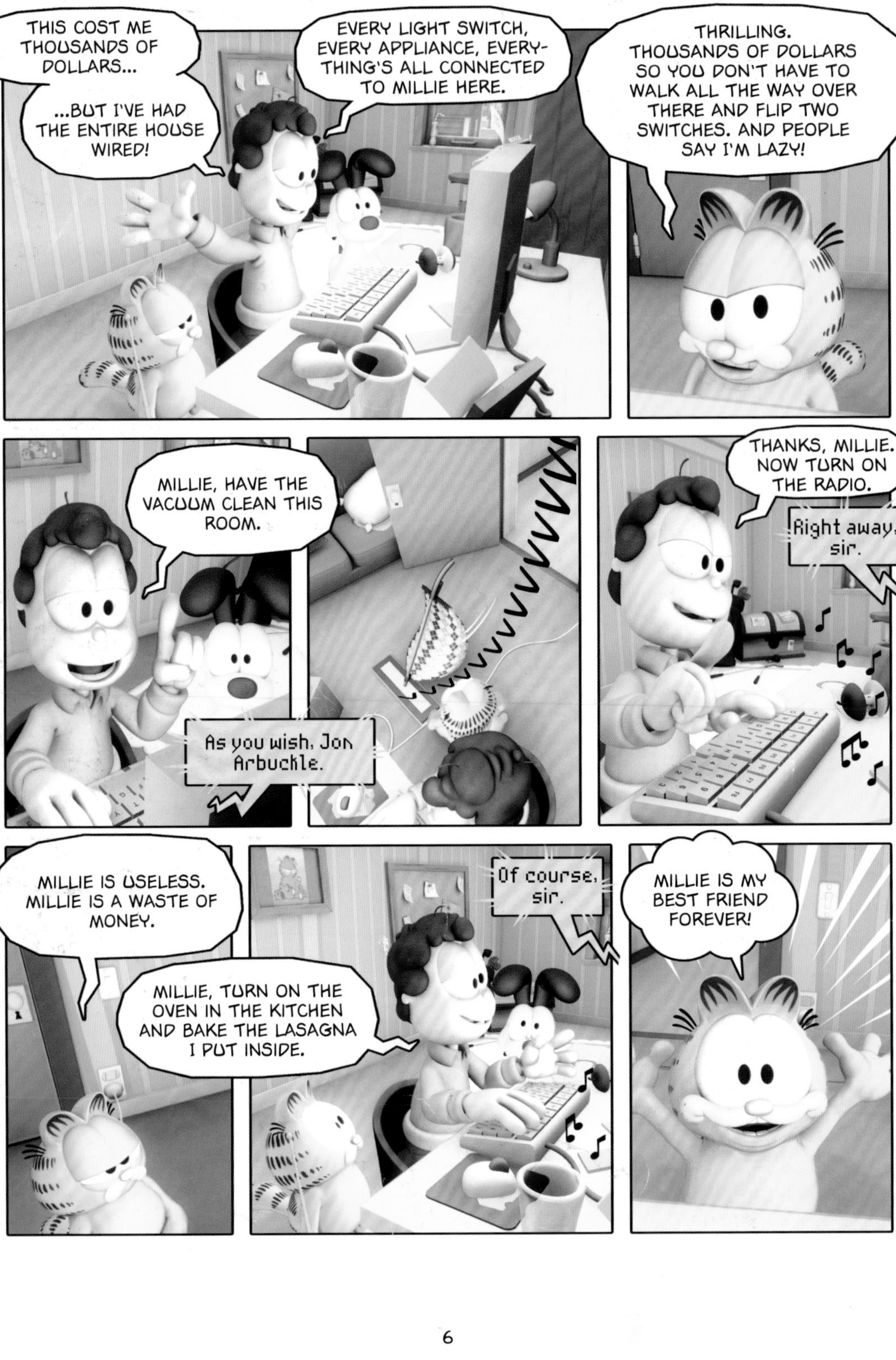
THIS COST ME THOUSANDS OF DOLLARS...
...BUT I'VE HAD THE ENTIRE HOUSE WIRED!
EVERY LIGHT SWITCH, EVERY APPLIANCE, EVERY-THING'S ALL CONNECTED TO MILLIE HERE.
THRILLING. THOUSANDS OF DOLLARS SO YOU DON'T HAVE TO WALK ALL THE WAY OVER THERE AND FLIP TWO SWITCHES. AND PEOPLE SAY I'M LAZY!
MILLIE, HAVE THE VACUUM CLEAN THIS ROOM.
As you wish, Jon Arbuckle.
VVVVVVVVVVVVVVVVVVV
THANKS, MILLIE. NOW TURN ON THE RADIO.
Right away, sir.
MILLIE IS USELESS. MILLIE IS A WASTE OF MONEY.
MILLIE, TURN ON THE OVEN IN THE KITCHEN AND BAKE THE LASAGNA I PUT INSIDE.
Of course, sir.
MILLIE IS MY BEST FRIEND FOREVER!

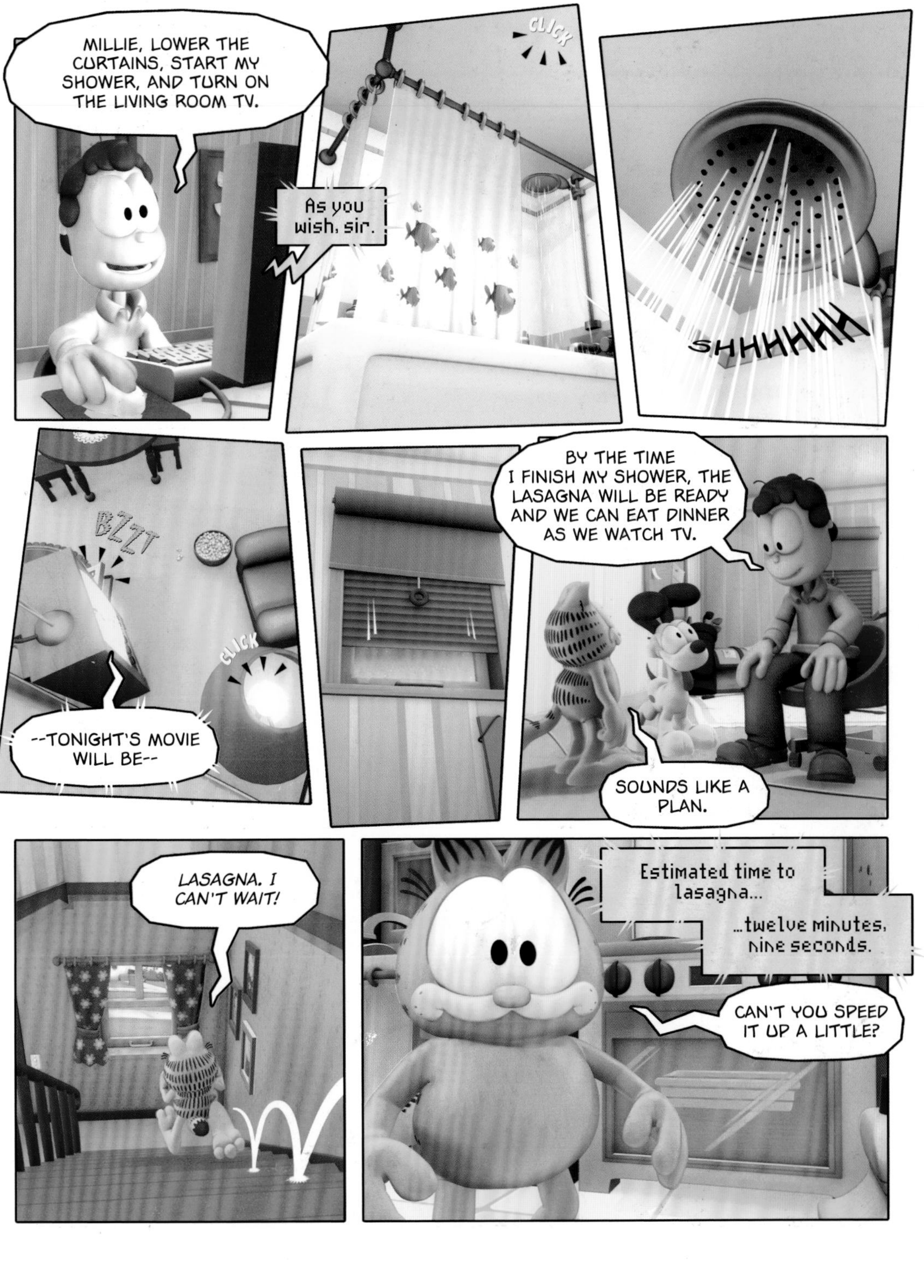
MILLIE, LOWER THE CURTAINS, START MY SHOWER, AND TURN ON THE LIVING ROOM TV.
CLICK
As you wish, sir.
SHHHHHH
BZZT
CLICK
--TONIGHT'S MOVIE WILL BE--
BY THE TIME I FINISH MY SHOWER, THE LASAGNA WILL BE READY AND WE CAN EAT DINNER AS WE WATCH TV.
SOUNDS LIKE A PLAN.
LASAGNA. I CAN'T WAIT!
Estimated time to lasagna...
...twelve minutes, nine seconds.
CAN'T YOU SPEED IT UP A LITTLE?

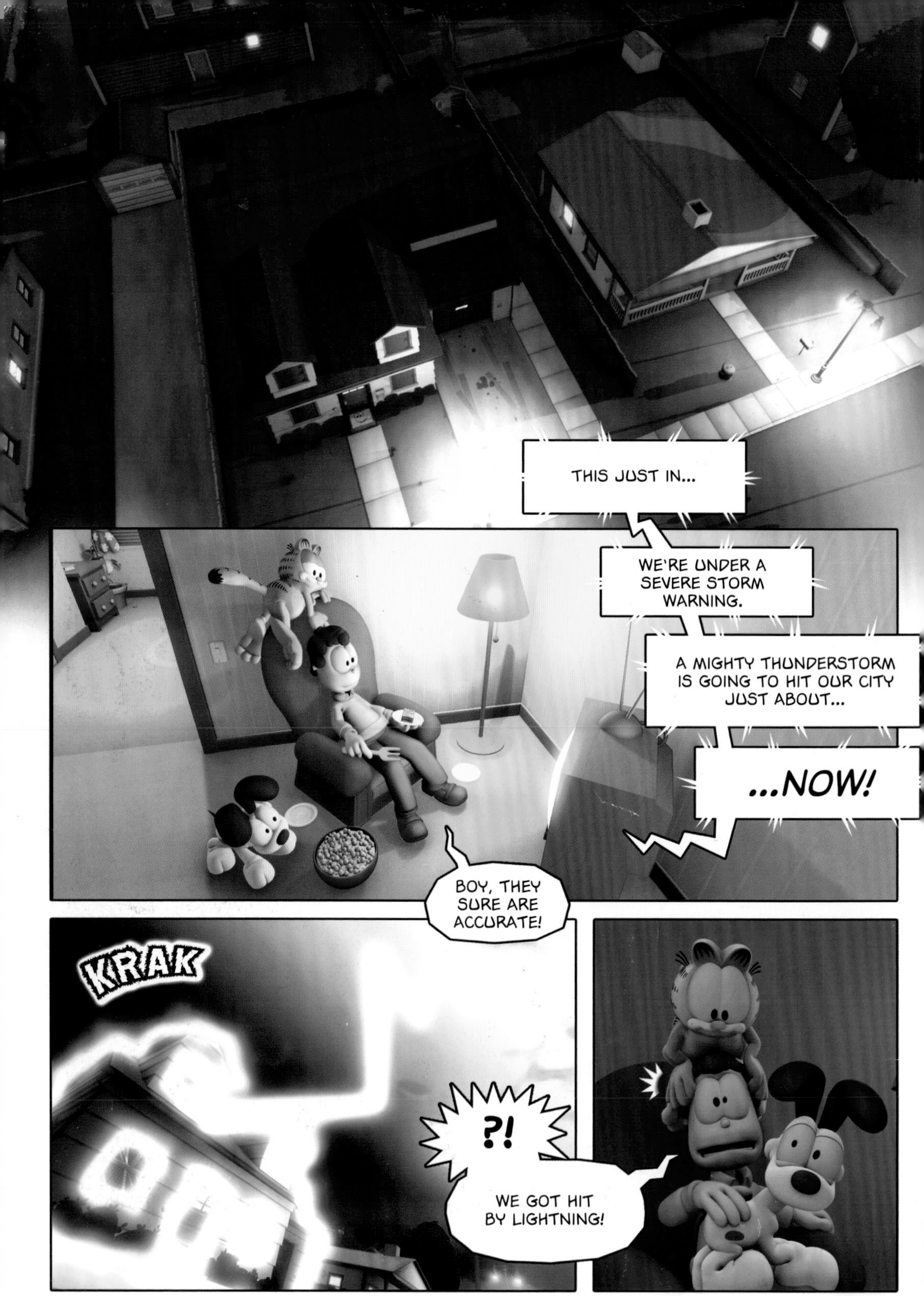
THIS JUST IN...
WE'RE UNDER A SEVERE STORM WARNING.
A MIGHTY THUNDERSTORM IS GOING TO HIT OUR CITY JUST ABOUT...
...NOW!
BOY, THEY SURE ARE ACCURATE!
KRAK
?!
WE GOT HIT BY LIGHTNING!

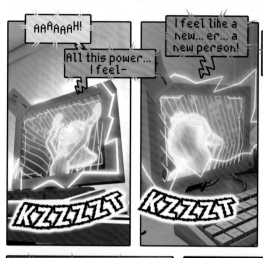

AAAAAAH!

All this power... I feel—

I feel like a new... er... a new person!

I have become superior, almighty!

I am an all-knowing being!

Now I'm in command!

HEY, WAIT! THIS IS MY HOUSE!

Not anymore!

CLICK

The appliances that I command are going to help me drive you and your animals out of MY house!

BZT

BZZZZT

Today, we will conquer this house. And tomorrow, the neighborhood. After that, the whole country...

--and then, the entire planet!

BUHWAHAHA!

BZT

BZZZZT

BZZZZT

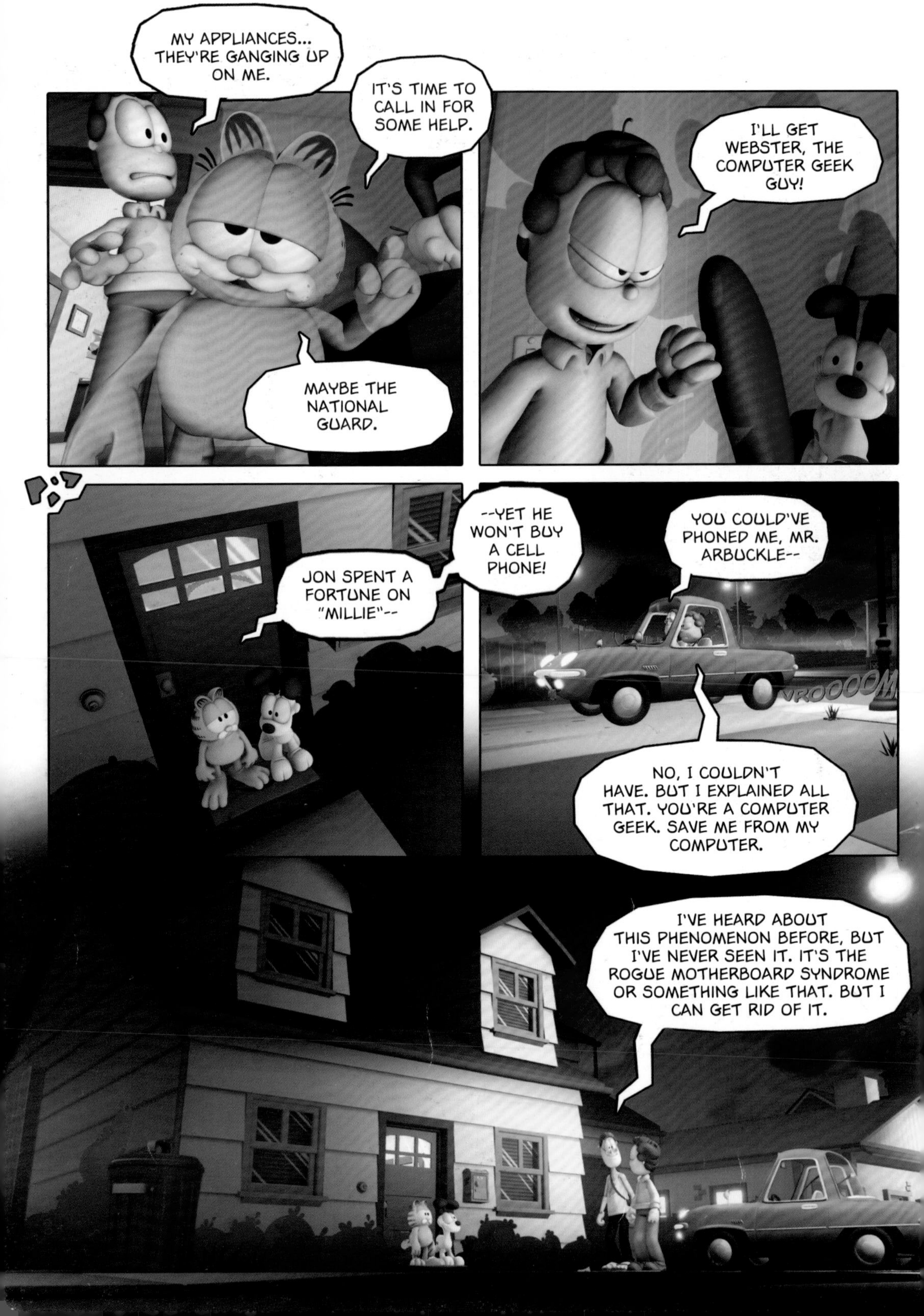
MY APPLIANCES... THEY'RE GANGING UP ON ME.
IT'S TIME TO CALL IN FOR SOME HELP.
MAYBE THE NATIONAL GUARD.
I'LL GET WEBSTER, THE COMPUTER GEEK GUY!
JON SPENT A FORTUNE ON "MILLIE"--
--YET HE WON'T BUY A CELL PHONE!
YOU COULD'VE PHONED ME, MR. ARBUCKLE--
VROOOOOM
NO, I COULDN'T HAVE. BUT I EXPLAINED ALL THAT. YOU'RE A COMPUTER GEEK. SAVE ME FROM MY COMPUTER.
I'VE HEARD ABOUT THIS PHENOMENON BEFORE, BUT I'VE NEVER SEEN IT. IT'S THE ROGUE MOTHERBOARD SYNDROME OR SOMETHING LIKE THAT. BUT I CAN GET RID OF IT.

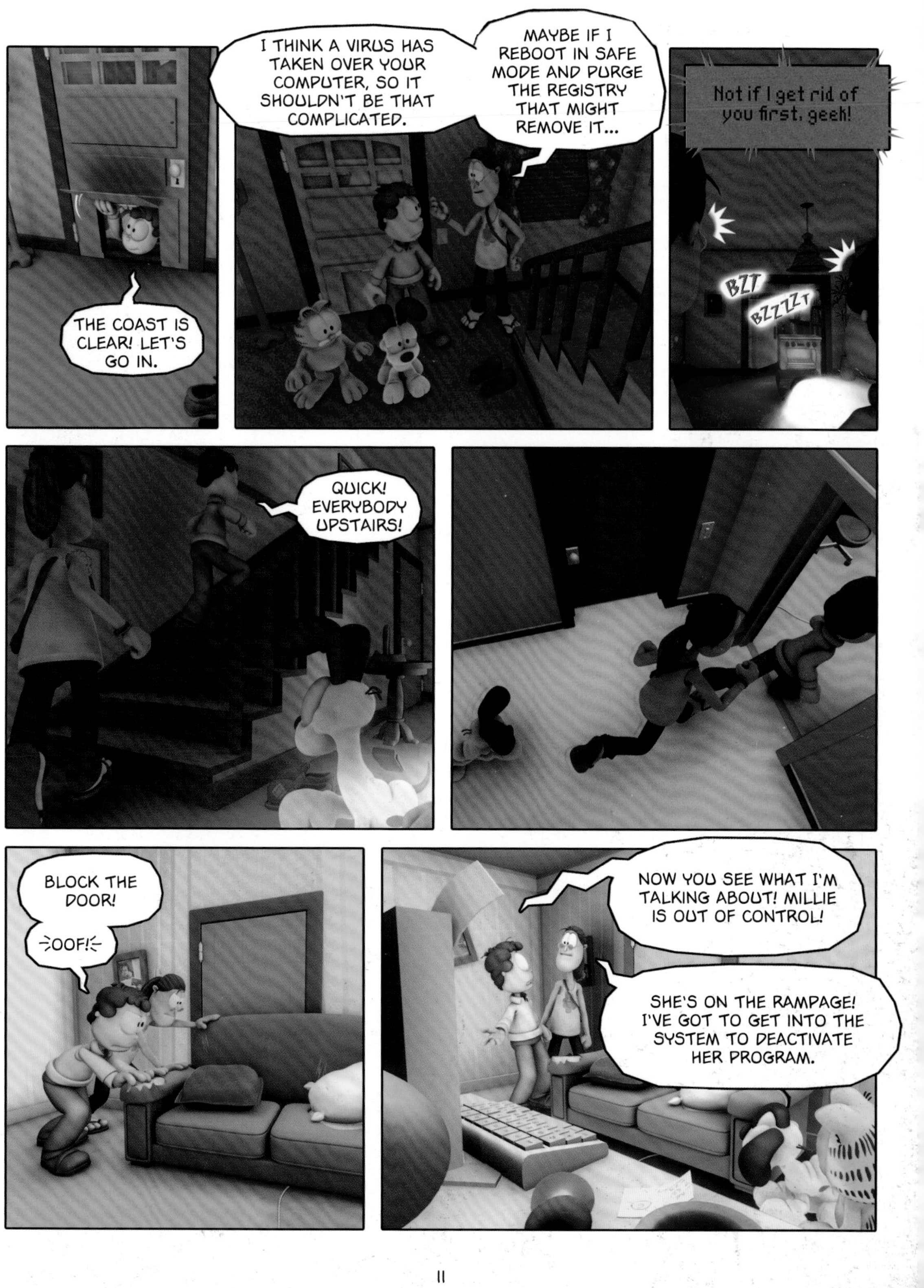
THE COAST IS CLEAR! LET'S GO IN.
I THINK A VIRUS HAS TAKEN OVER YOUR COMPUTER, SO IT SHOULDN'T BE THAT COMPLICATED.
MAYBE IF I REBOOT IN SAFE MODE AND PURGE THE REGISTRY THAT MIGHT REMOVE IT...
Not if I get rid of you first, geek!
BZT
BZZZZT
QUICK! EVERYBODY UPSTAIRS!
BLOCK THE DOOR!
OOF!
NOW YOU SEE WHAT I'M TALKING ABOUT! MILLIE IS OUT OF CONTROL!
SHE'S ON THE RAMPAGE! I'VE GOT TO GET INTO THE SYSTEM TO DEACTIVATE HER PROGRAM.

THE SYSTEM'S UP AND RUNNING...

...BUT SOMETHING'S BLOCKING MY ACCESS.

Ha, ha, ha!

I've reinforced the system to protect myself!

TAP TAP TAP TAP TAP TAP TAP

THERE ARE WAYS AROUND THAT.

You're wasting your time, geek!

WEBSTER! DO SOMETHING!

NOTHING I'VE TRIED IS WORKING!

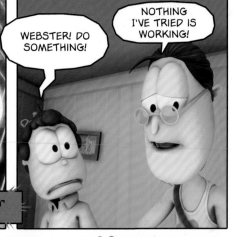

MILLIE HAS SHUT DOWN ALL ACCESS TO HER PROGRAM.

TOO LATE!

BLAM

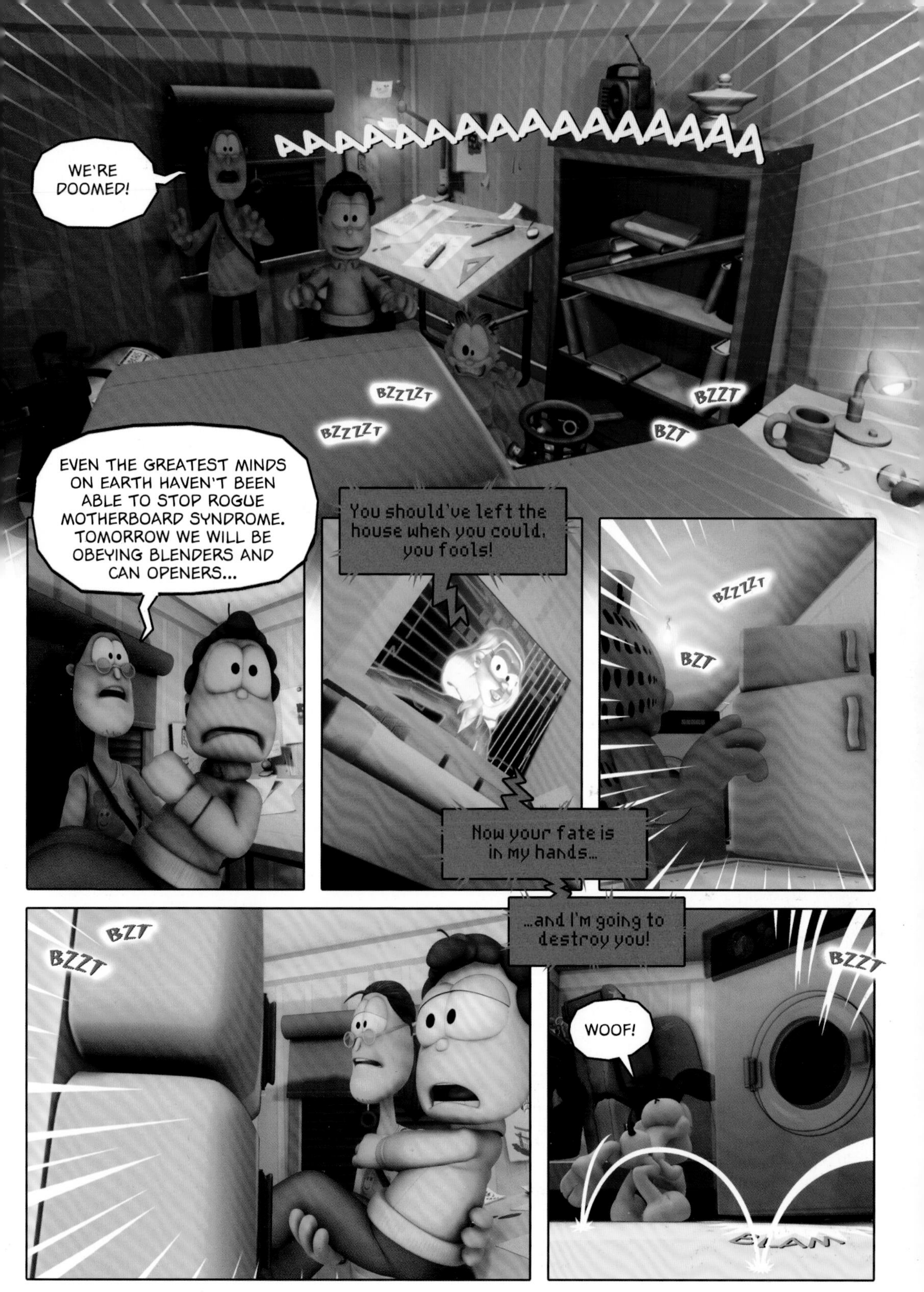
WE'RE DOOMED!
AAAAAAAAAAAAAAAA
BZZZZT
BZZZZT
BZZT
BZT
EVEN THE GREATEST MINDS ON EARTH HAVEN'T BEEN ABLE TO STOP ROGUE MOTHERBOARD SYNDROME. TOMORROW WE WILL BE OBEYING BLENDERS AND CAN OPENERS...
You should've left the house when you could, you fools!
BZZZZT
BZT
Now your fate is in my hands...
...and I'm going to destroy you!
BZT
BZZZT
BZZZT
WOOF!
BLAM

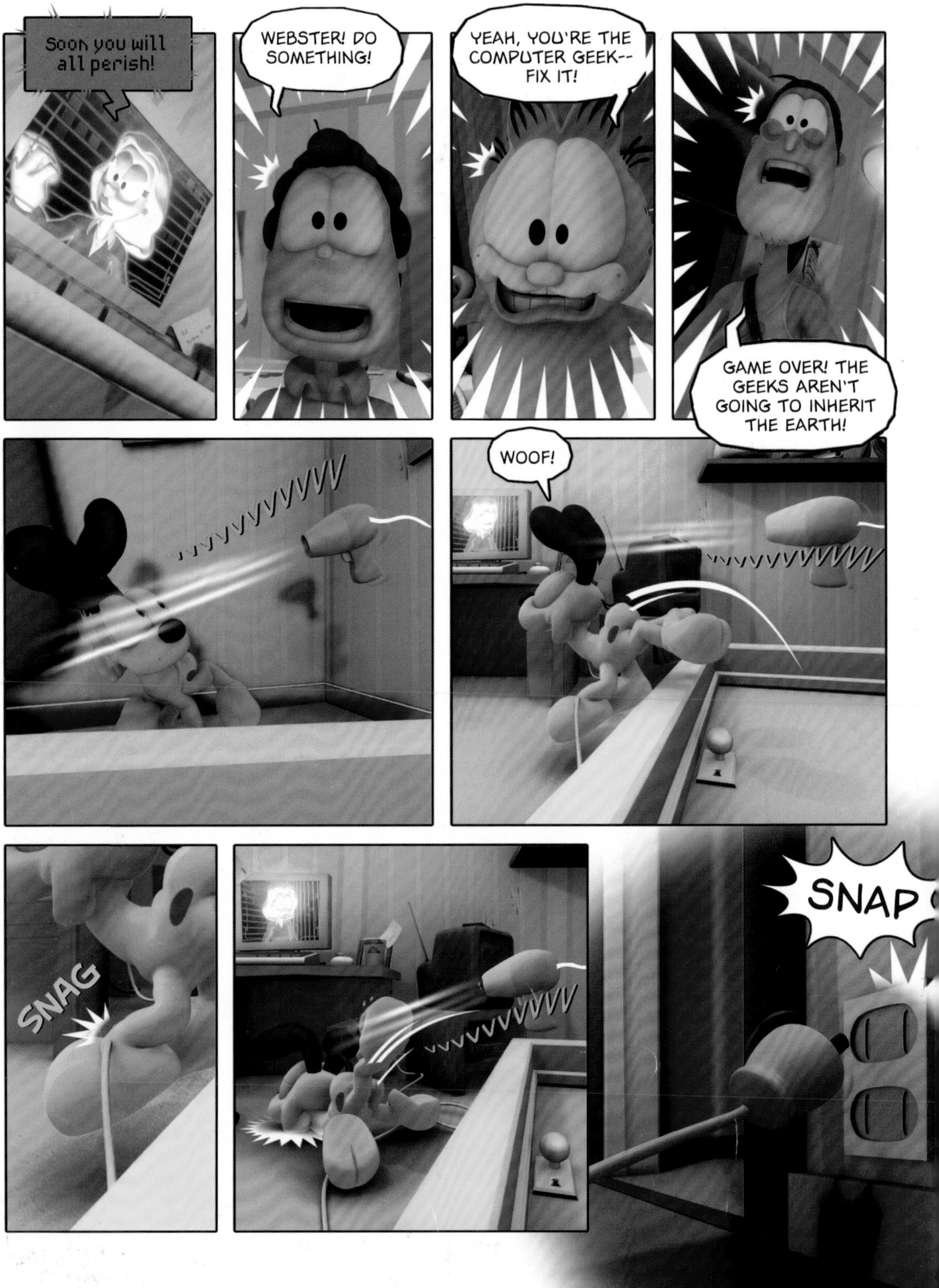
Soon you will all perish!
WEBSTER! DO SOMETHING!
YEAH, YOU'RE THE COMPUTER GEEK-- FIX IT!
GAME OVER! THE GEEKS AREN'T GOING TO INHERIT THE EARTH!
VVVVVVVVVVVVVV
WOOF!
VVVVVVVVVVVVV
SNAG
VVVVVVVVVVV
SNAP

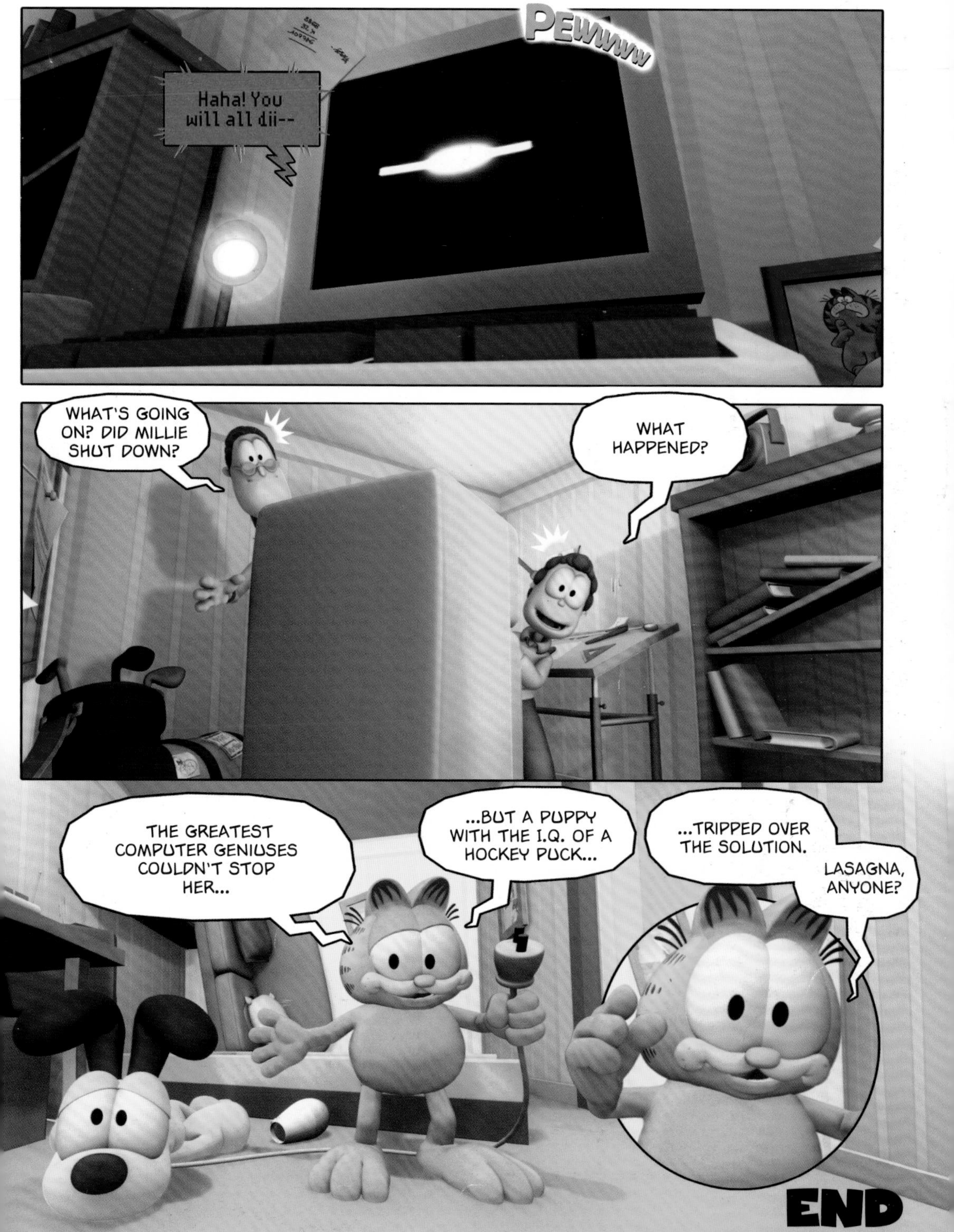

PEWWWW
Haha! You will all dii--
WHAT'S GOING ON? DID MILLIE SHUT DOWN?
WHAT HAPPENED?
THE GREATEST COMPUTER GENIUSES COULDN'T STOP HER...
...BUT A PUPPY WITH THE I.Q. OF A HOCKEY PUCK...
...TRIPPED OVER THE SOLUTION.
LASAGNA, ANYONE?
END

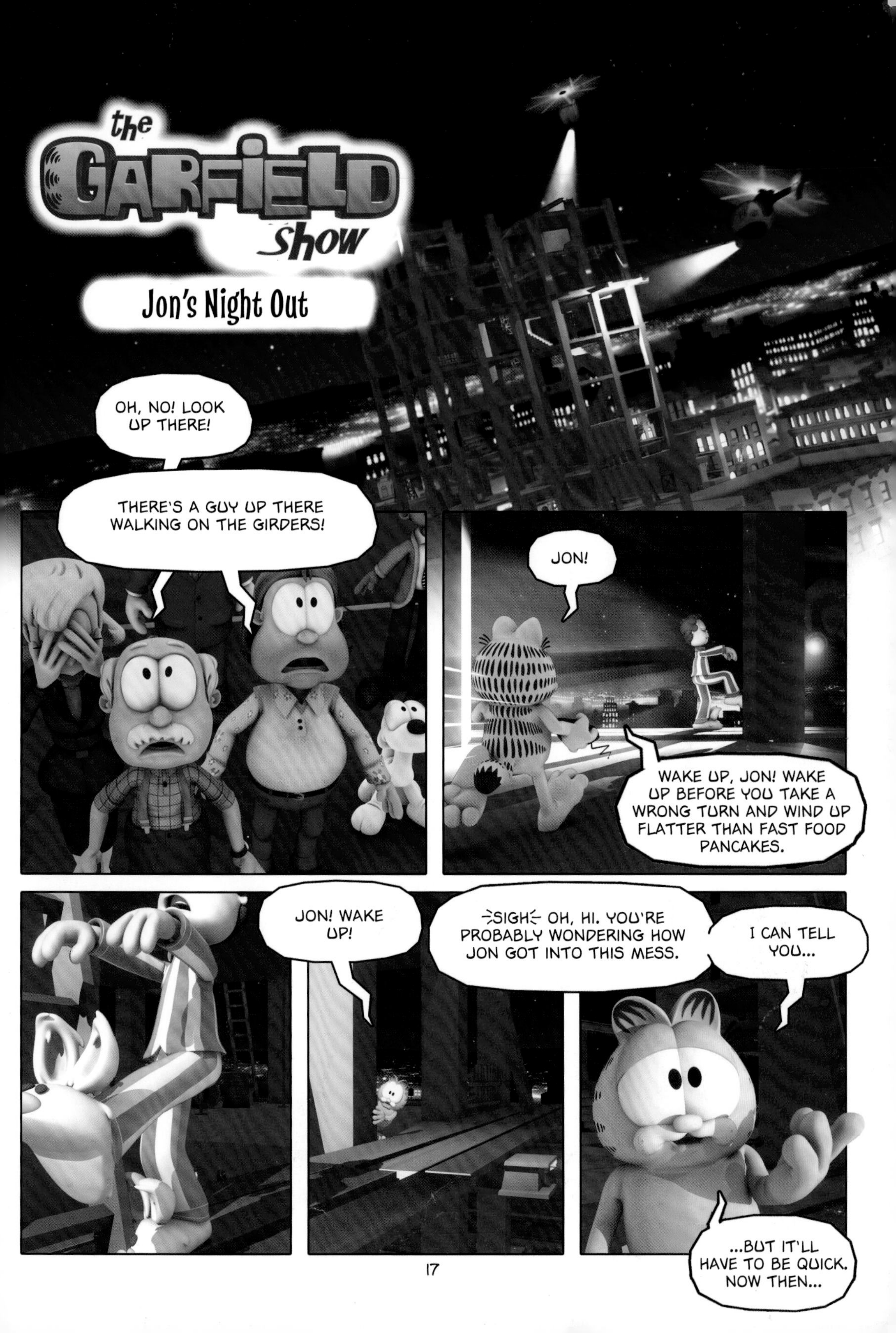
the GARFIELD show
Jon's Night Out
OH, NO! LOOK UP THERE!
THERE'S A GUY UP THERE WALKING ON THE GIRDERS!
JON!
WAKE UP, JON! WAKE UP BEFORE YOU TAKE A WRONG TURN AND WIND UP FLATTER THAN FAST FOOD PANCAKES.
JON! WAKE UP!
SIGH OH, HI. YOU'RE PROBABLY WONDERING HOW JON GOT INTO THIS MESS.
I CAN TELL YOU...
...BUT IT'LL HAVE TO BE QUICK. NOW THEN...

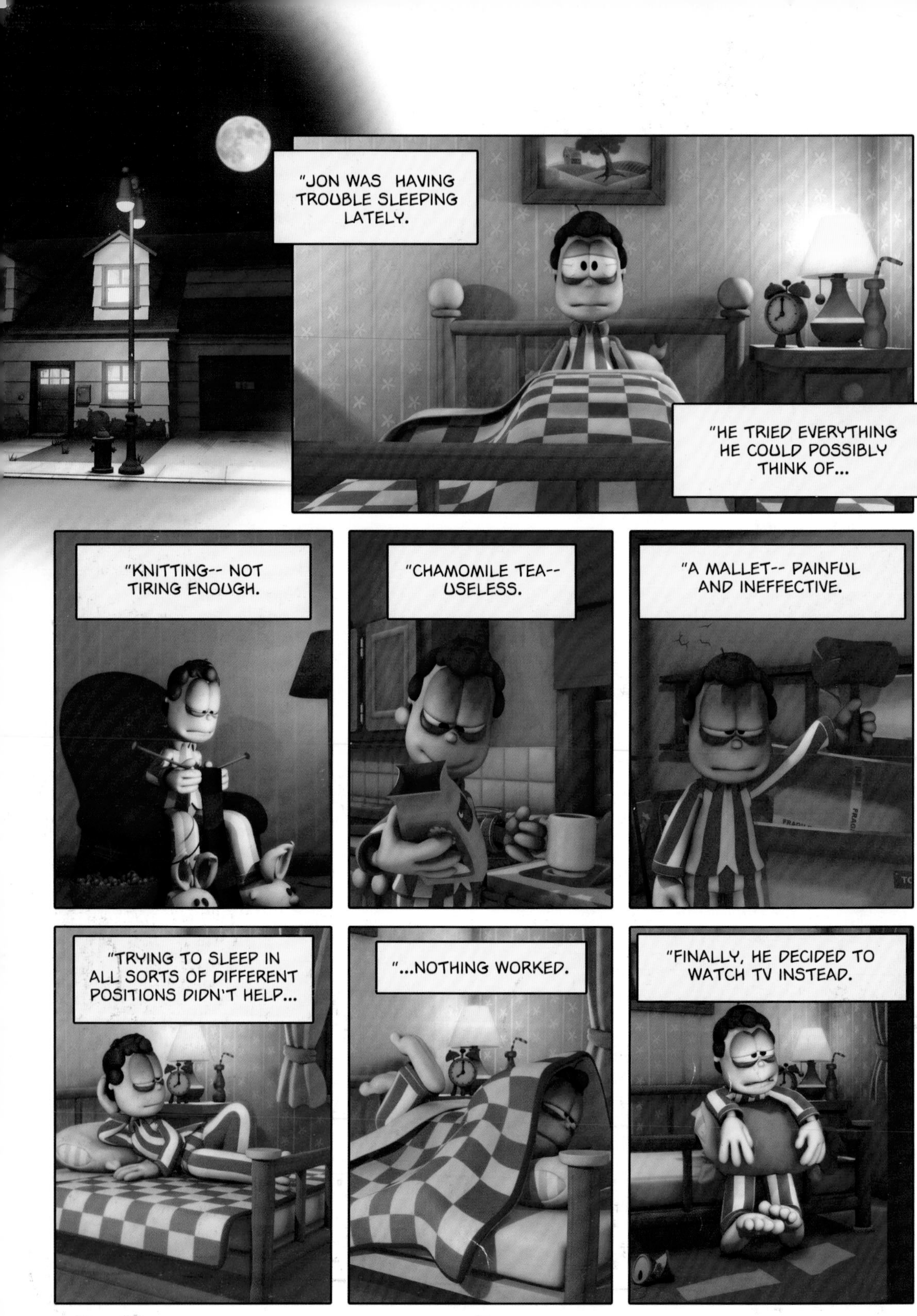
"JON WAS HAVING TROUBLE SLEEPING LATELY.
"HE TRIED EVERYTHING HE COULD POSSIBLY THINK OF...
"KNITTING-- NOT TIRING ENOUGH.
"CHAMOMILE TEA-- USELESS.
"A MALLET-- PAINFUL AND INEFFECTIVE.
"TRYING TO SLEEP IN ALL SORTS OF DIFFERENT POSITIONS DIDN'T HELP...
"...NOTHING WORKED.
"FINALLY, HE DECIDED TO WATCH TV INSTEAD.

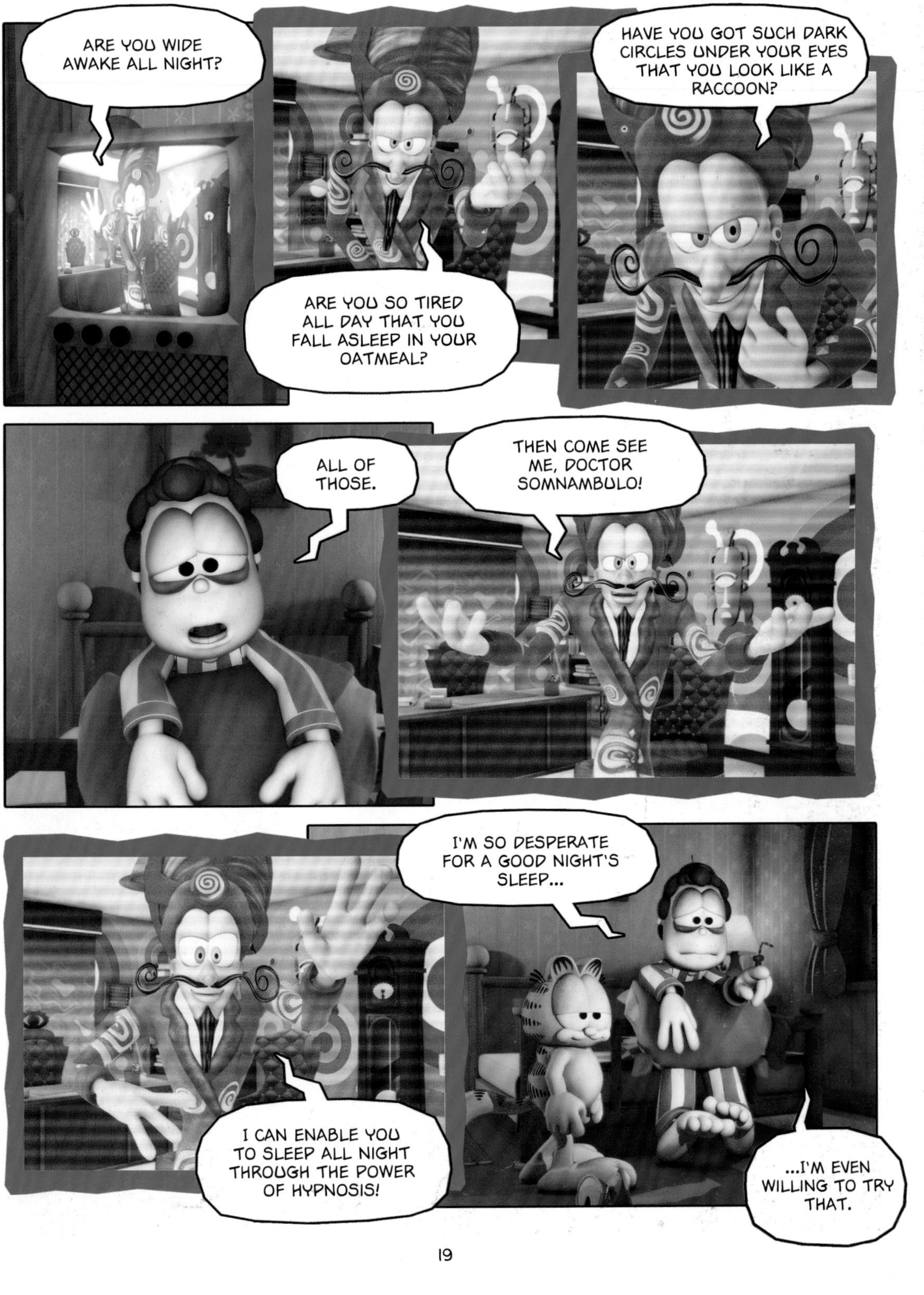
ARE YOU WIDE AWAKE ALL NIGHT?
ARE YOU SO TIRED ALL DAY THAT YOU FALL ASLEEP IN YOUR OATMEAL?
HAVE YOU GOT SUCH DARK CIRCLES UNDER YOUR EYES THAT YOU LOOK LIKE A RACCOON?
ALL OF THOSE.
THEN COME SEE ME, DOCTOR SOMNAMBULO!
I CAN ENABLE YOU TO SLEEP ALL NIGHT THROUGH THE POWER OF HYPNOSIS!
I'M SO DESPERATE FOR A GOOD NIGHT'S SLEEP...
...I'M EVEN WILLING TO TRY THAT.

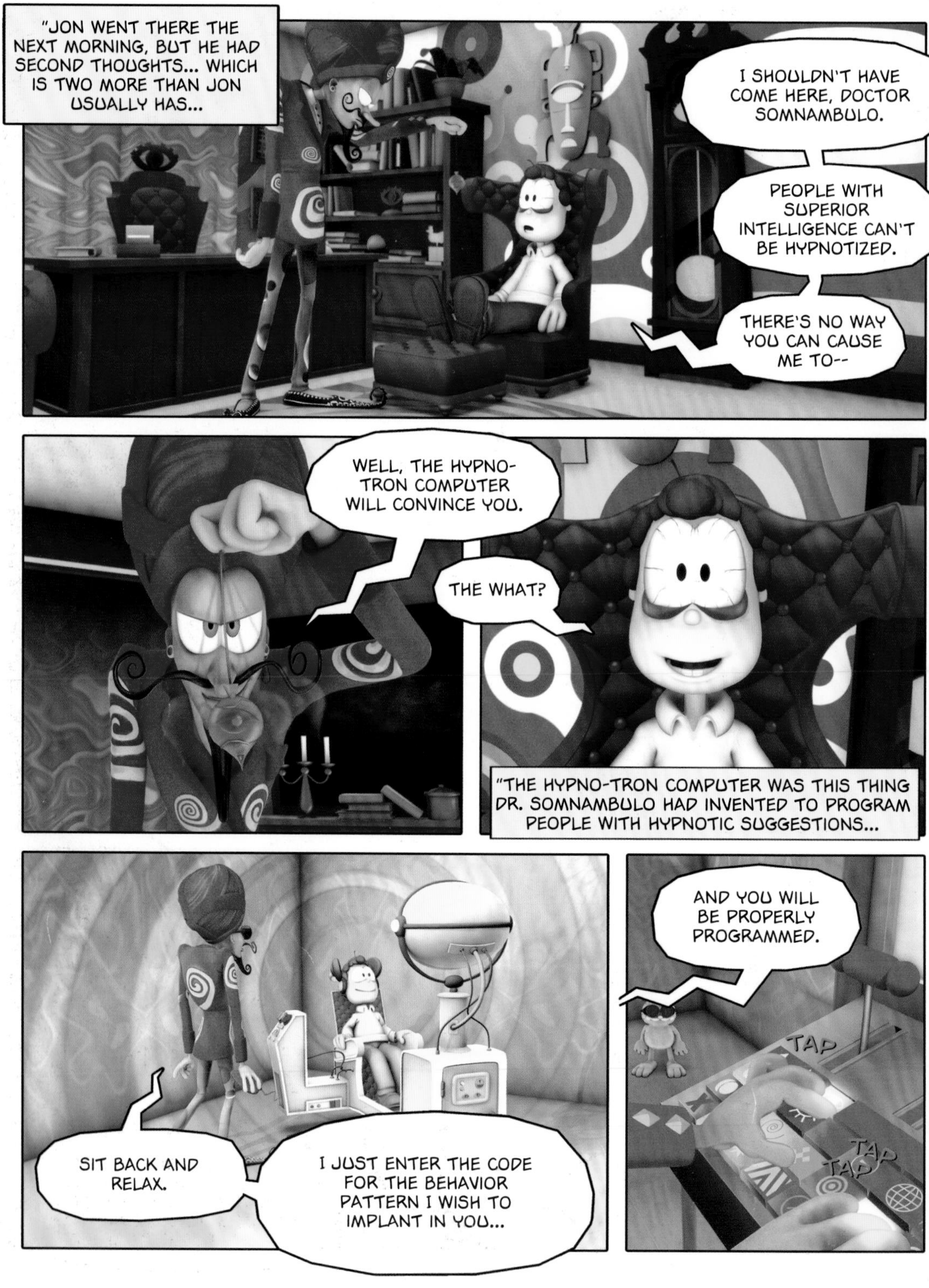
"JON WENT THERE THE NEXT MORNING, BUT HE HAD SECOND THOUGHTS... WHICH IS TWO MORE THAN JON USUALLY HAS...
I SHOULDN'T HAVE COME HERE, DOCTOR SOMNAMBULO.
PEOPLE WITH SUPERIOR INTELLIGENCE CAN'T BE HYPNOTIZED.
THERE'S NO WAY YOU CAN CAUSE ME TO--
WELL, THE HYPNO-TRON COMPUTER WILL CONVINCE YOU.
THE WHAT?
"THE HYPNO-TRON COMPUTER WAS THIS THING DR. SOMNAMBULO HAD INVENTED TO PROGRAM PEOPLE WITH HYPNOTIC SUGGESTIONS...
SIT BACK AND RELAX.
I JUST ENTER THE CODE FOR THE BEHAVIOR PATTERN I WISH TO IMPLANT IN YOU...
AND YOU WILL BE PROPERLY PROGRAMMED.
TAP
TAP
TAP

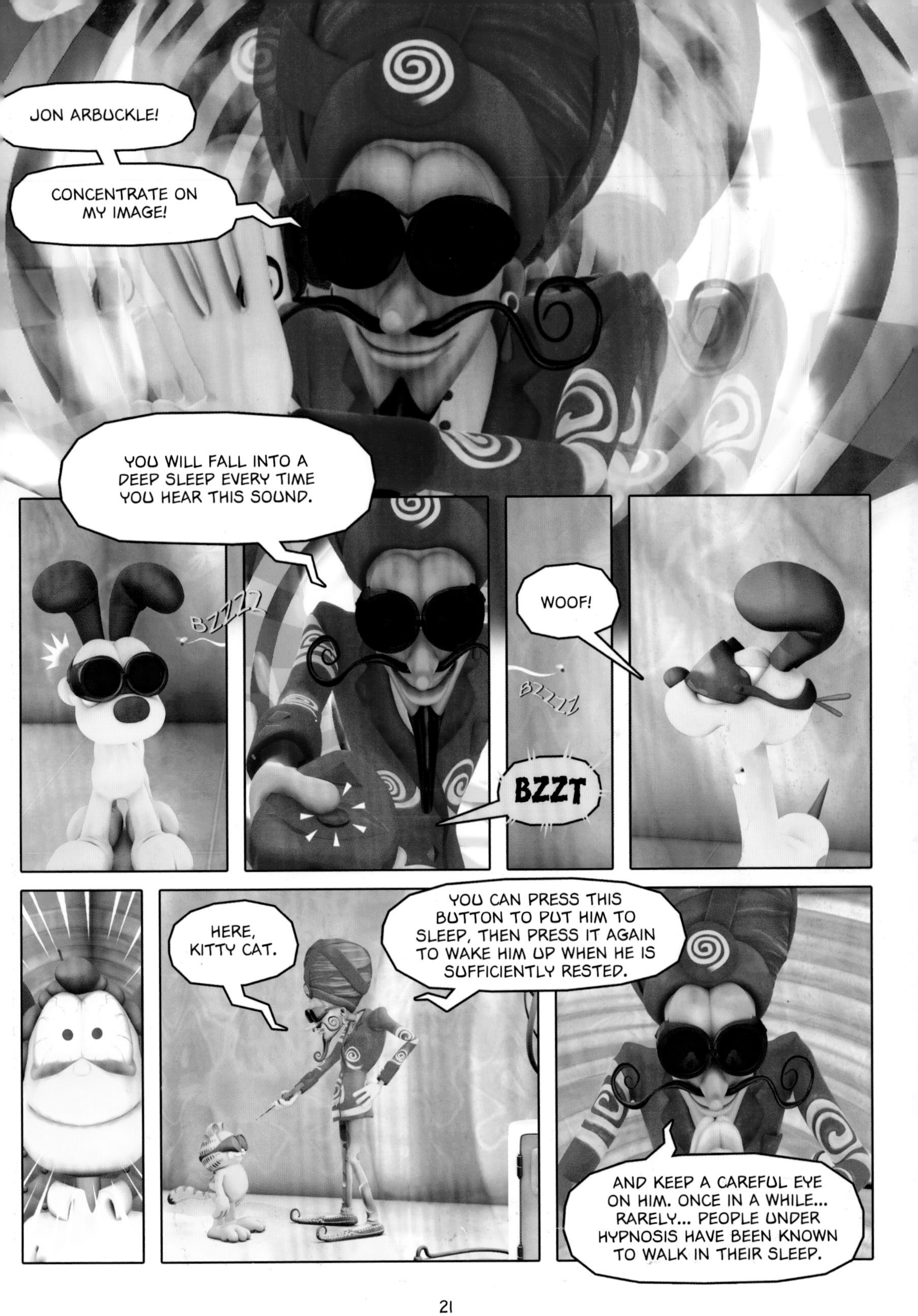
JON ARBUCKLE!
CONCENTRATE ON MY IMAGE!
YOU WILL FALL INTO A DEEP SLEEP EVERY TIME YOU HEAR THIS SOUND.
BZZZZ
BZZT
BZZZZ
WOOF!
HERE, KITTY CAT.
YOU CAN PRESS THIS BUTTON TO PUT HIM TO SLEEP, THEN PRESS IT AGAIN TO WAKE HIM UP WHEN HE IS SUFFICIENTLY RESTED.
AND KEEP A CAREFUL EYE ON HIM. ONCE IN A WHILE... RARELY... PEOPLE UNDER HYPNOSIS HAVE BEEN KNOWN TO WALK IN THEIR SLEEP.

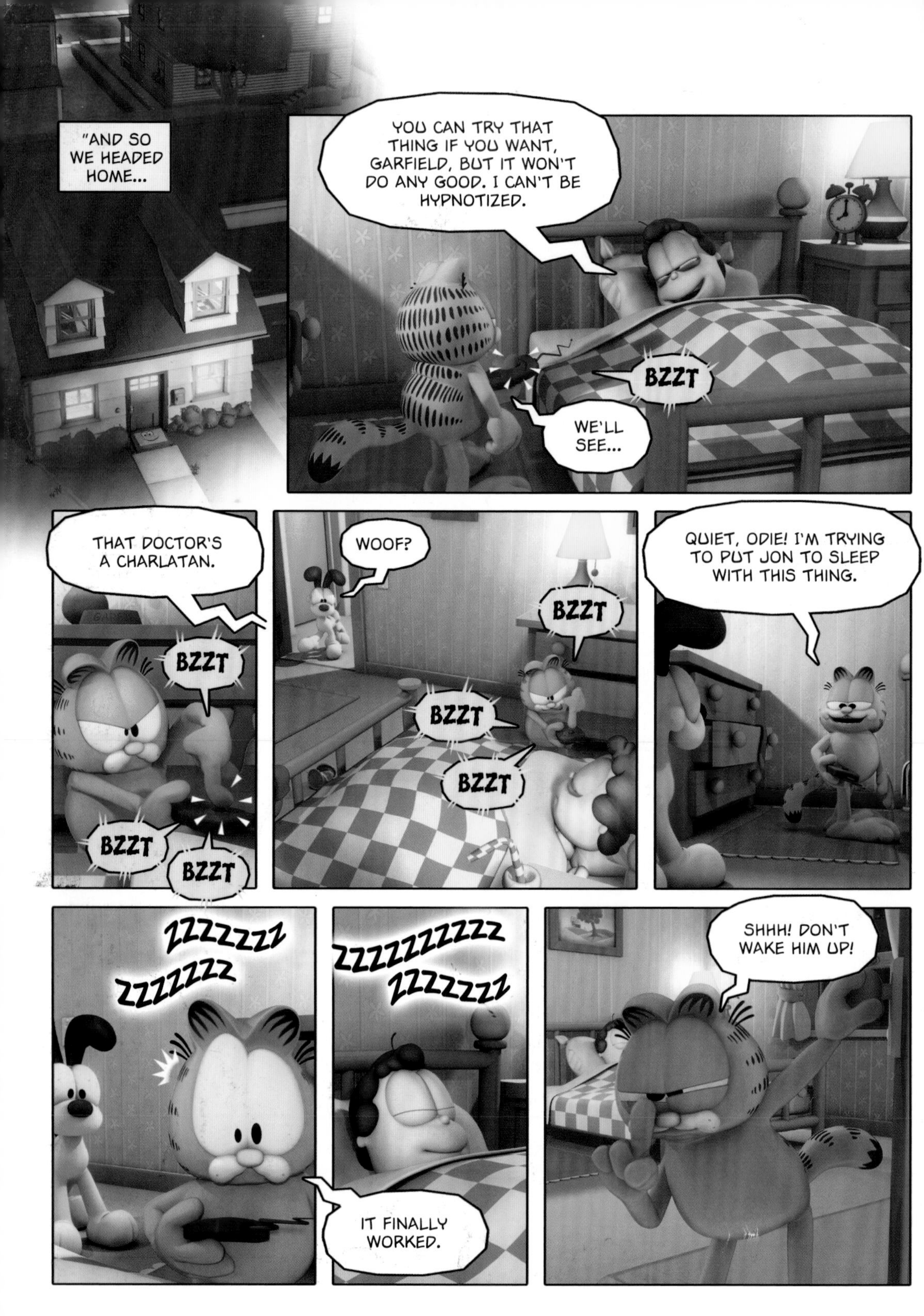
"AND SO WE HEADED HOME...
YOU CAN TRY THAT THING IF YOU WANT, GARFIELD, BUT IT WON'T DO ANY GOOD. I CAN'T BE HYPNOTIZED.
BZZT
WE'LL SEE...
THAT DOCTOR'S A CHARLATAN.
BZZT
BZZT
BZZT
WOOF?
BZZT
BZZT
BZZT
QUIET, ODIE! I'M TRYING TO PUT JON TO SLEEP WITH THIS THING.
ZZZZZZZ
ZZZZZZZ
ZZZZZZZZZZ
ZZZZZZZ
IT FINALLY WORKED.
SHHH! DON'T WAKE HIM UP!

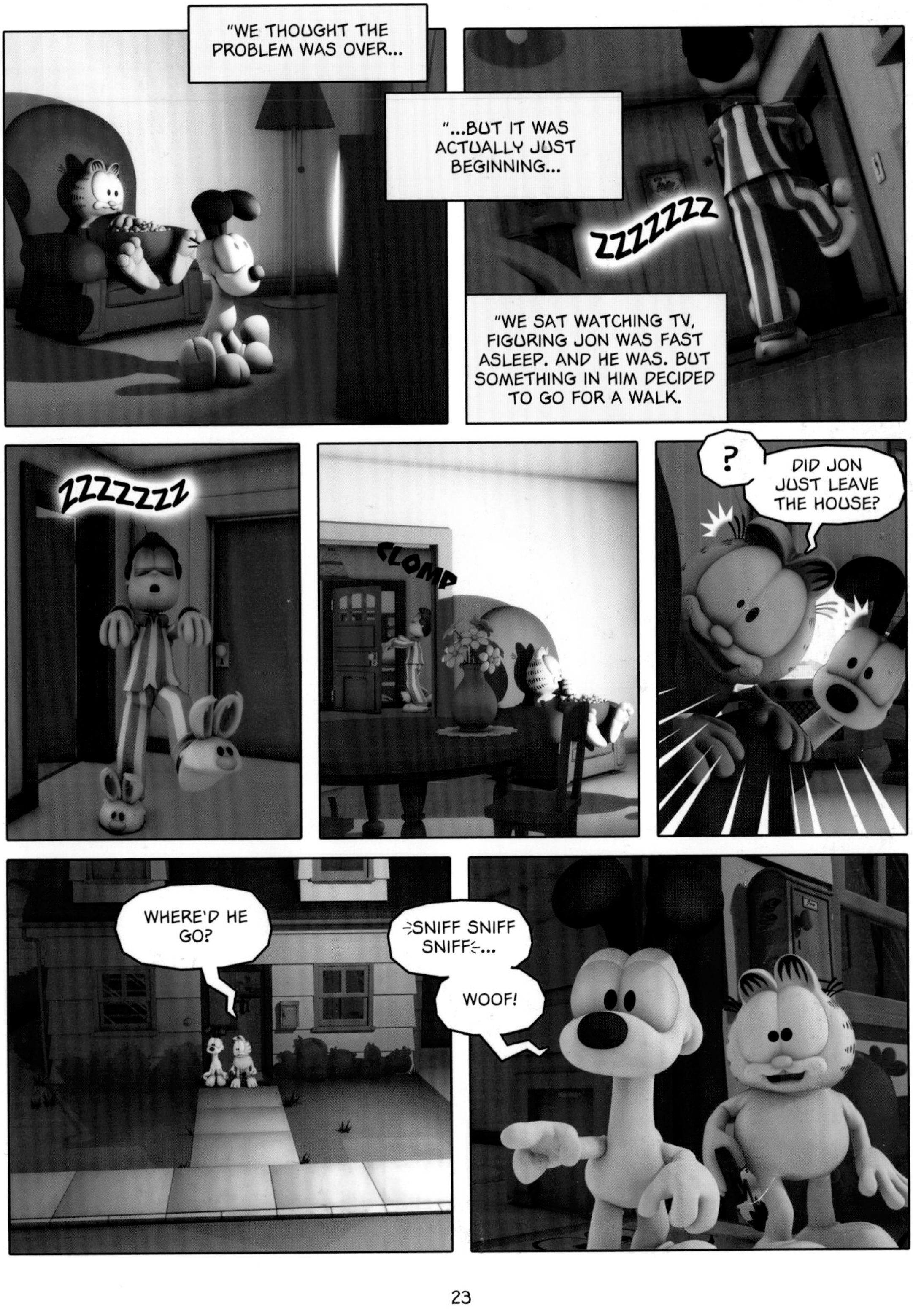
"WE THOUGHT THE PROBLEM WAS OVER...
"...BUT IT WAS ACTUALLY JUST BEGINNING...
ZZZZZZZ
"WE SAT WATCHING TV, FIGURING JON WAS FAST ASLEEP. AND HE WAS. BUT SOMETHING IN HIM DECIDED TO GO FOR A WALK.
ZZZZZZZ
CLOMP
?
DID JON JUST LEAVE THE HOUSE?
WHERE'D HE GO?
SNIFF SNIFF SNIFF...
WOOF!

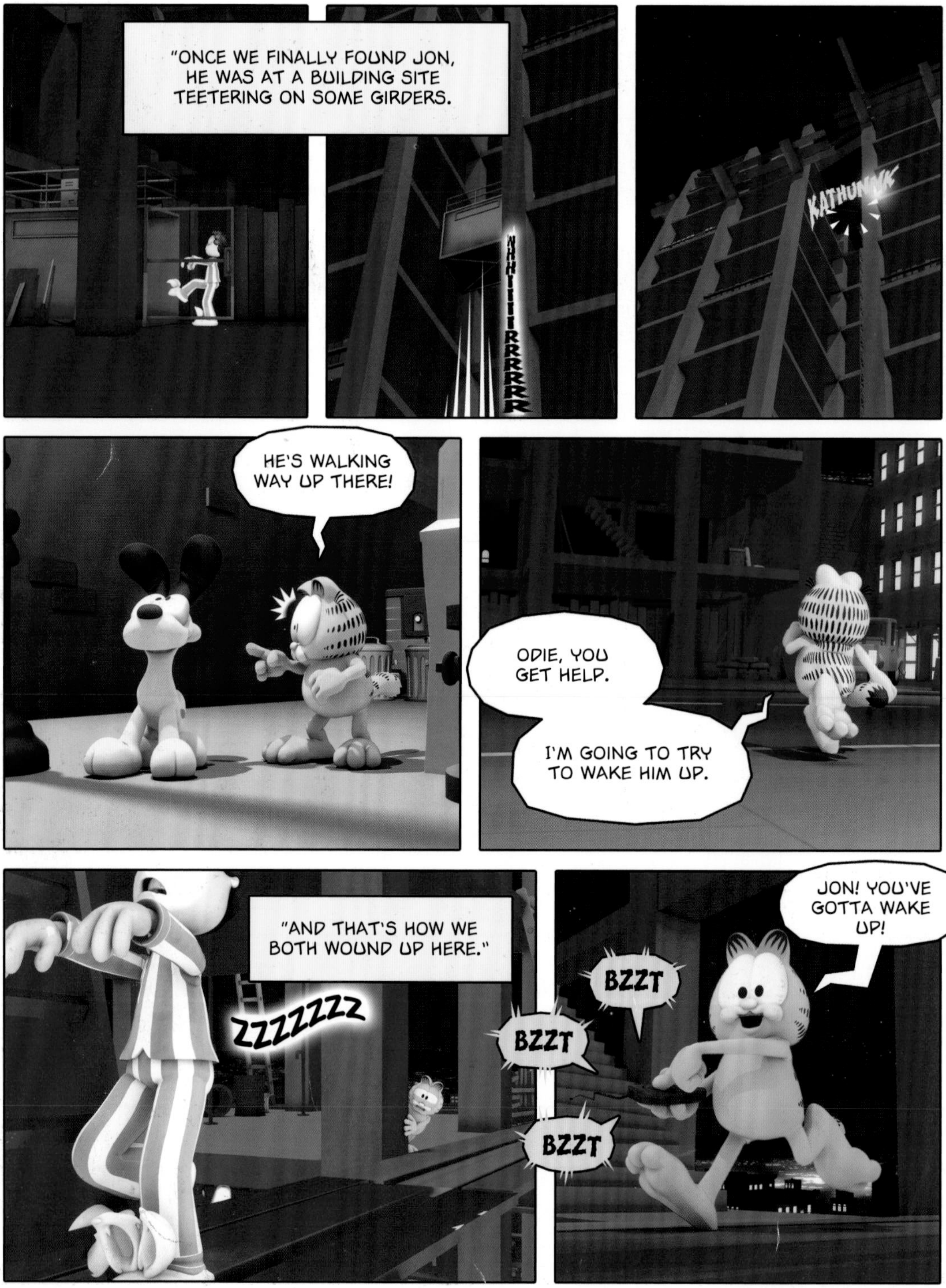
"ONCE WE FINALLY FOUND JON, HE WAS AT A BUILDING SITE TEETERING ON SOME GIRDERS.
WHHIIIIIRRRRRR
KATHUNK
HE'S WALKING WAY UP THERE!
ODIE, YOU GET HELP.
I'M GOING TO TRY TO WAKE HIM UP.
"AND THAT'S HOW WE BOTH WOUND UP HERE."
ZZZZZZZ
BZZT
BZZT
BZZT
JON! YOU'VE GOTTA WAKE UP!

ZZZZZZ

OH, NO!

THE TROUBLE IS I KEEP BUZZING THIS BUZZER AND IT DOESN'T WAKE HIM UP.

WHAT'S HE DOING UP THERE?

WOOF!

BZZT

IT'S SO DANGEROUS!

BZZT

BZZT BZZT

HUH?

WOOF!

ZZZZZZ ZZZZZZ

WOOF!

HUH?

WOOF!

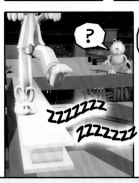   

?

ZZZZZZ ZZZZZZ

"AT THAT MOMENT, I FINALLY UNDERSTOOD WHAT HAD HAPPENED.

ODIE'S BARKING IS WAKING JON UP AND PUTTING HIM TO SLEEP.

ODIE! BARK ONE MORE TIME!

WOOF!

HUH?

WHAT'S GOING ON?

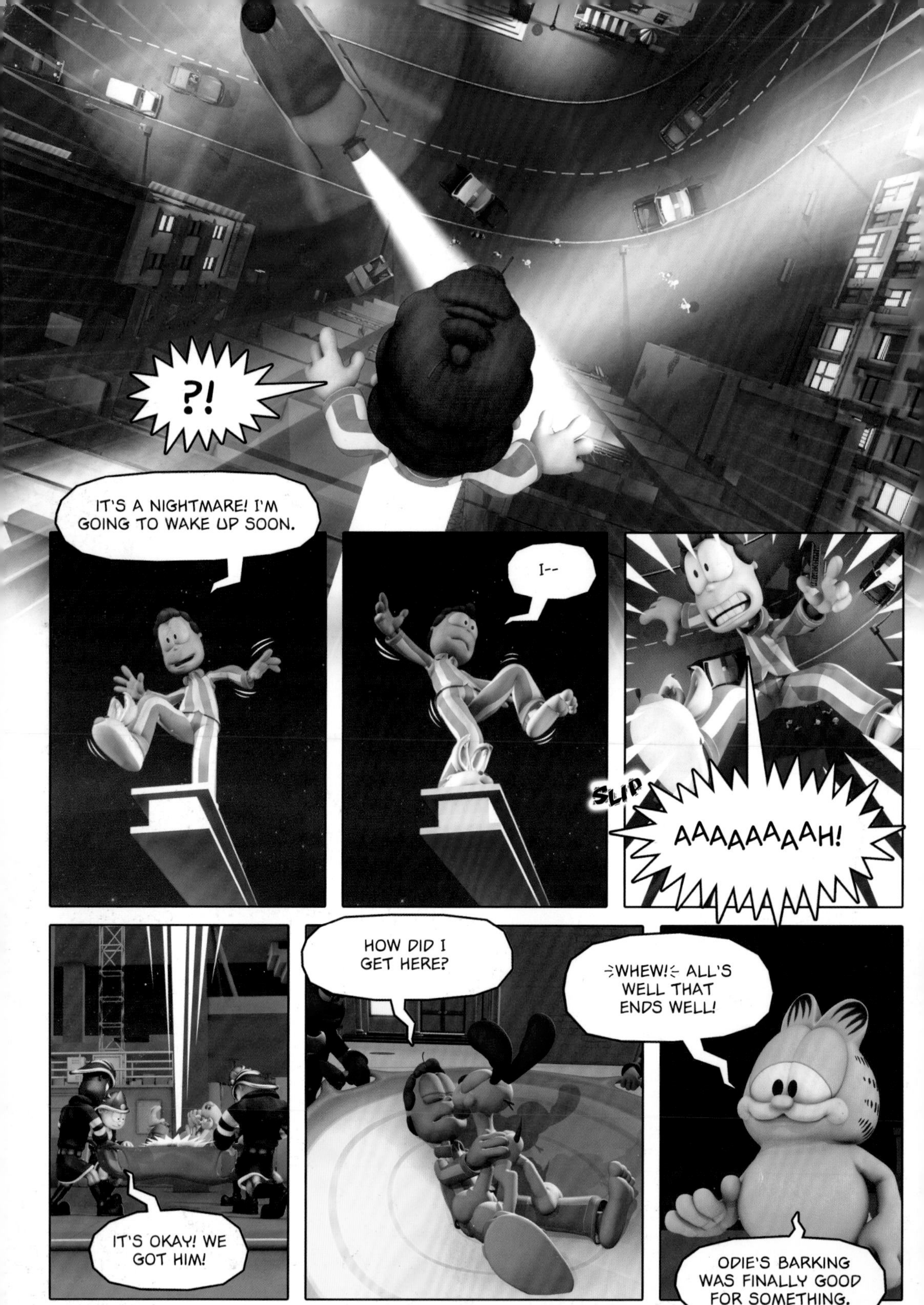
?!
IT'S A NIGHTMARE! I'M GOING TO WAKE UP SOON.
I--
SLIP
AAAAAAAAH!
IT'S OKAY! WE GOT HIM!
HOW DID I GET HERE?
WHEW! ALL'S WELL THAT ENDS WELL!
ODIE'S BARKING WAS FINALLY GOOD FOR SOMETHING.

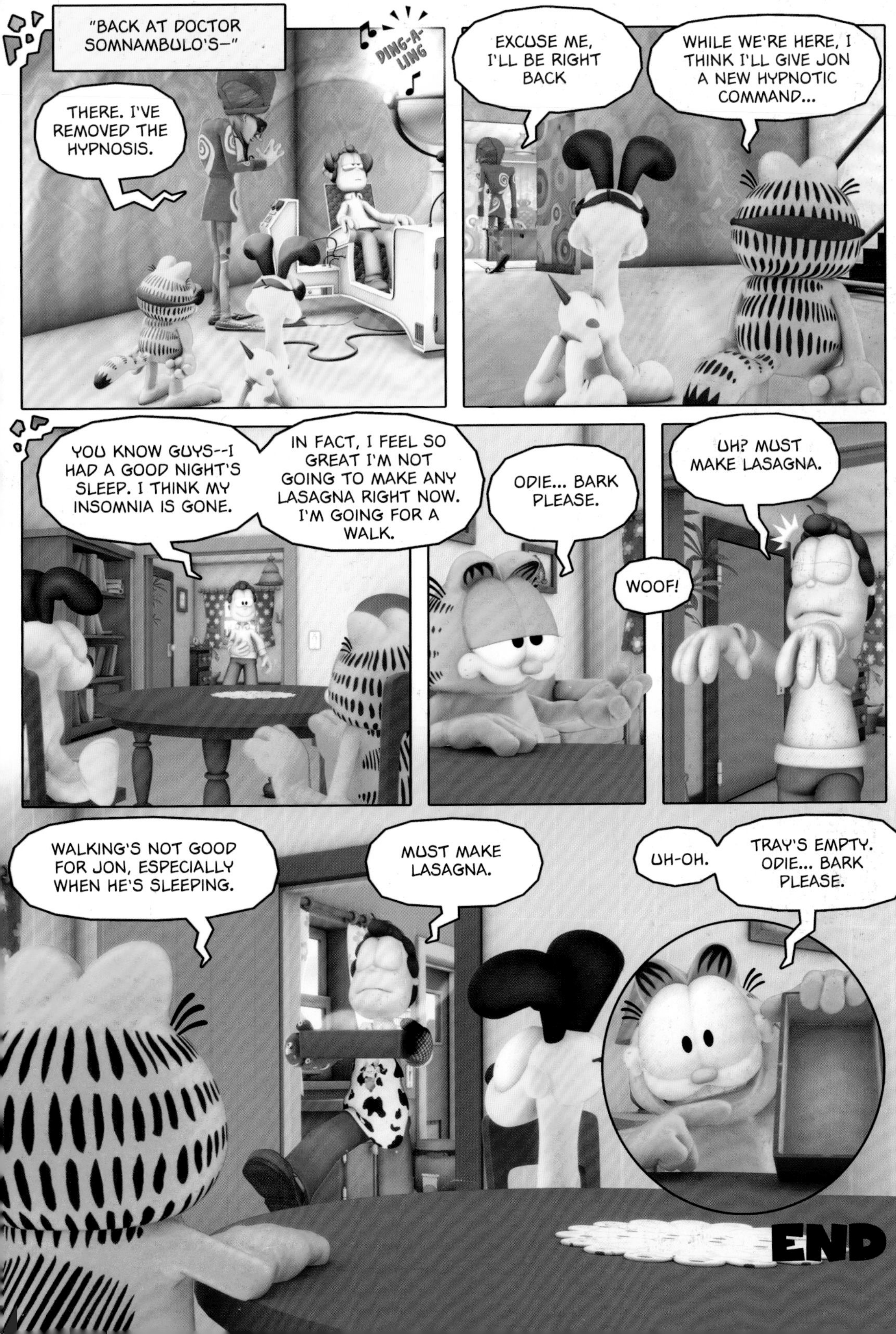
"BACK AT DOCTOR SOMNAMBULO'S--"
DING-A-LING
THERE. I'VE REMOVED THE HYPNOSIS.
EXCUSE ME, I'LL BE RIGHT BACK
WHILE WE'RE HERE, I THINK I'LL GIVE JON A NEW HYPNOTIC COMMAND...
YOU KNOW GUYS--I HAD A GOOD NIGHT'S SLEEP. I THINK MY INSOMNIA IS GONE.
IN FACT, I FEEL SO GREAT I'M NOT GOING TO MAKE ANY LASAGNA RIGHT NOW. I'M GOING FOR A WALK.
ODIE... BARK PLEASE.
WOOF!
UH? MUST MAKE LASAGNA.
WALKING'S NOT GOOD FOR JON, ESPECIALLY WHEN HE'S SLEEPING.
MUST MAKE LASAGNA.
UH-OH.
TRAY'S EMPTY. ODIE... BARK PLEASE.
END

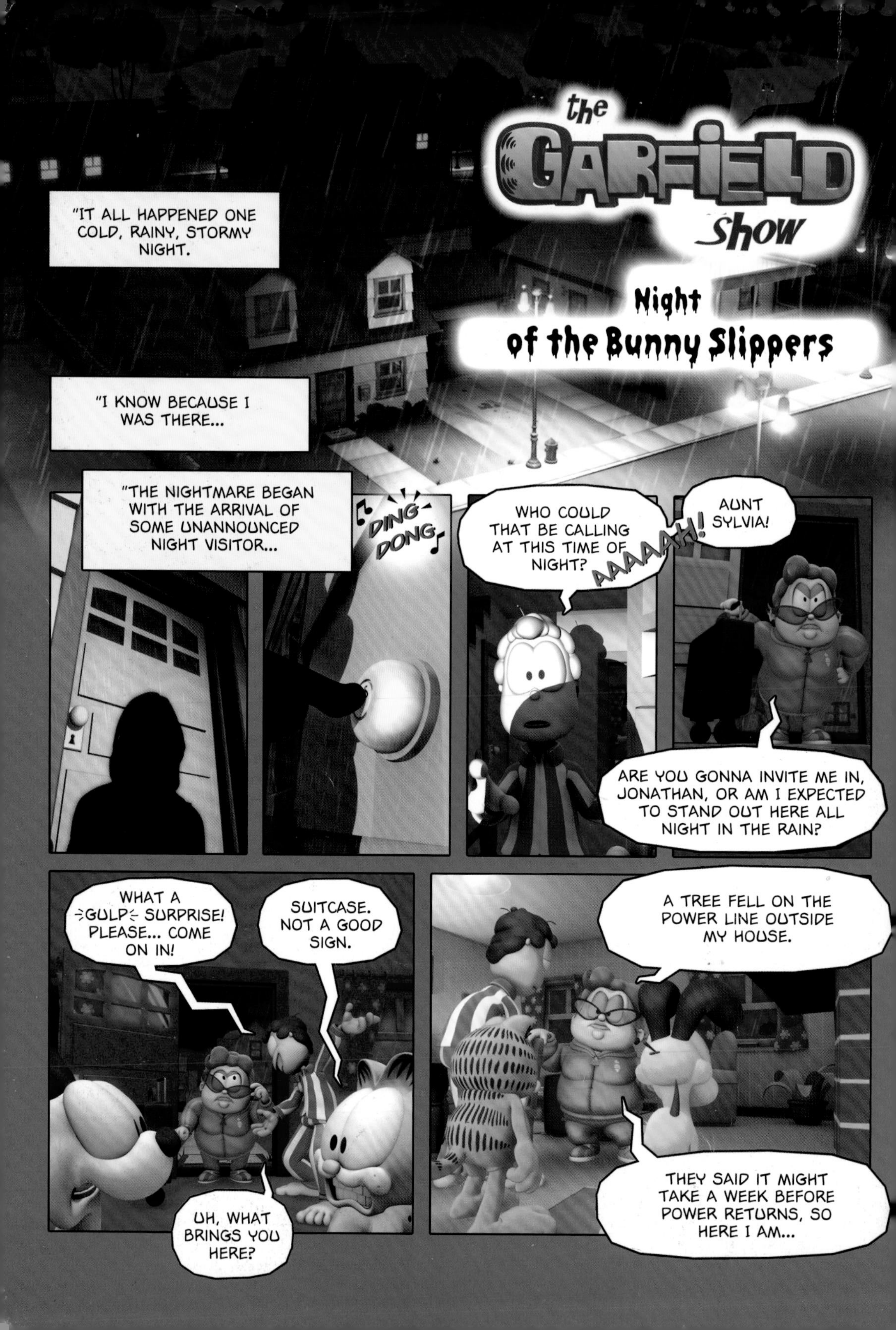
the GARFIELD show
Night of the Bunny Slippers
"IT ALL HAPPENED ONE COLD, RAINY, STORMY NIGHT.
"I KNOW BECAUSE I WAS THERE...
"THE NIGHTMARE BEGAN WITH THE ARRIVAL OF SOME UNANNOUNCED NIGHT VISITOR...
DING-DONG
WHO COULD THAT BE CALLING AT THIS TIME OF NIGHT?
AAAAAH!
AUNT SYLVIA!
ARE YOU GONNA INVITE ME IN, JONATHAN, OR AM I EXPECTED TO STAND OUT HERE ALL NIGHT IN THE RAIN?
WHAT A -GULP- SURPRISE! PLEASE... COME ON IN!
SUITCASE. NOT A GOOD SIGN.
UH, WHAT BRINGS YOU HERE?
A TREE FELL ON THE POWER LINE OUTSIDE MY HOUSE.
THEY SAID IT MIGHT TAKE A WEEK BEFORE POWER RETURNS, SO HERE I AM...

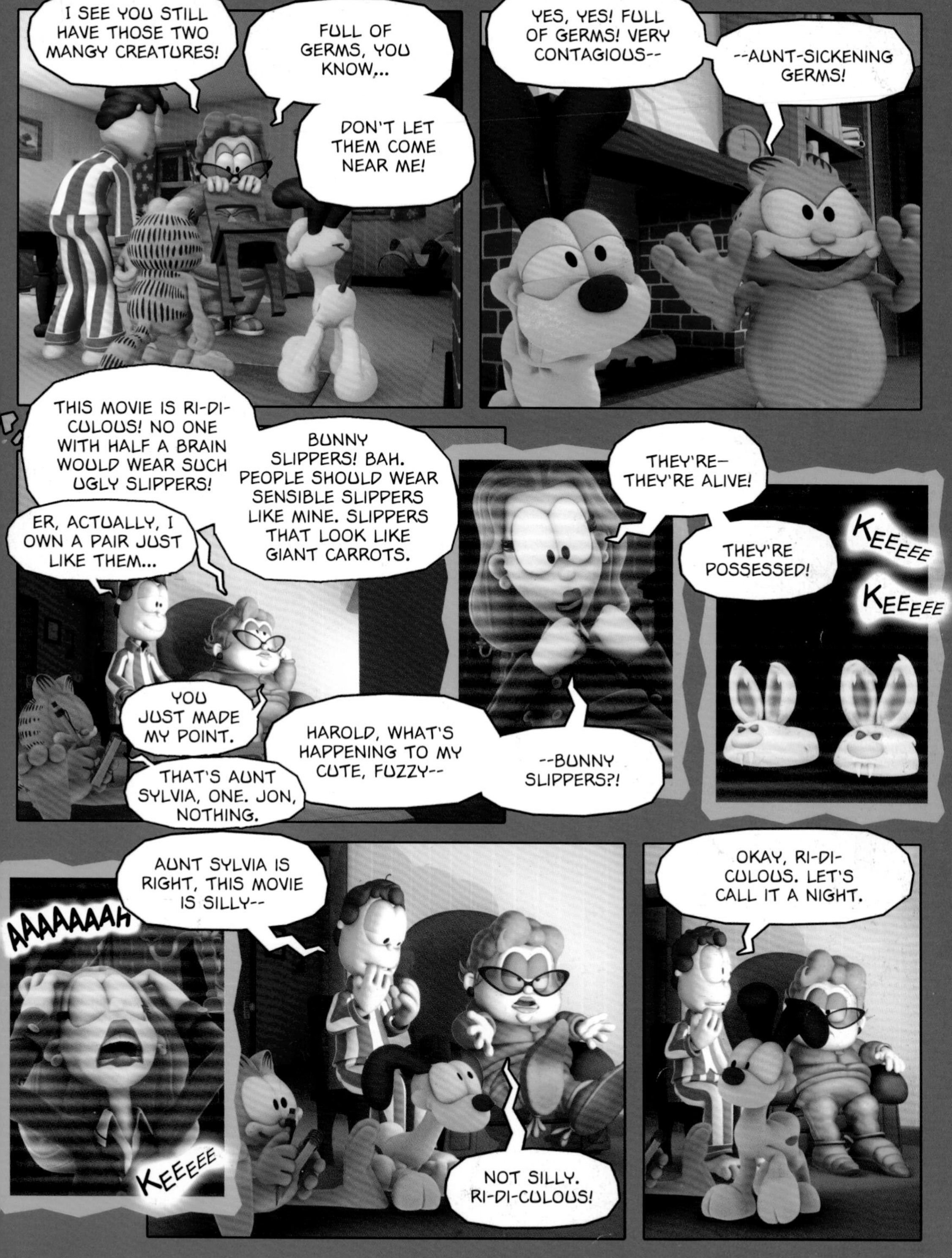
I SEE YOU STILL HAVE THOSE TWO MANGY CREATURES!
FULL OF GERMS, YOU KNOW,...
DON'T LET THEM COME NEAR ME!
YES, YES! FULL OF GERMS! VERY CONTAGIOUS--
--AUNT-SICKENING GERMS!
THIS MOVIE IS RI-DI-CULOUS! NO ONE WITH HALF A BRAIN WOULD WEAR SUCH UGLY SLIPPERS!
ER, ACTUALLY, I OWN A PAIR JUST LIKE THEM...
BUNNY SLIPPERS! BAH. PEOPLE SHOULD WEAR SENSIBLE SLIPPERS LIKE MINE. SLIPPERS THAT LOOK LIKE GIANT CARROTS.
YOU JUST MADE MY POINT.
THAT'S AUNT SYLVIA, ONE. JON, NOTHING.
THEY'RE— THEY'RE ALIVE!
HAROLD, WHAT'S HAPPENING TO MY CUTE, FUZZY--
--BUNNY SLIPPERS?!
THEY'RE POSSESSED!
KEEEEE
KEEEEE
AAAAAAAH
KEEEEE
AUNT SYLVIA IS RIGHT, THIS MOVIE IS SILLY--
NOT SILLY. RI-DI-CULOUS!
OKAY, RI-DI-CULOUS. LET'S CALL IT A NIGHT.

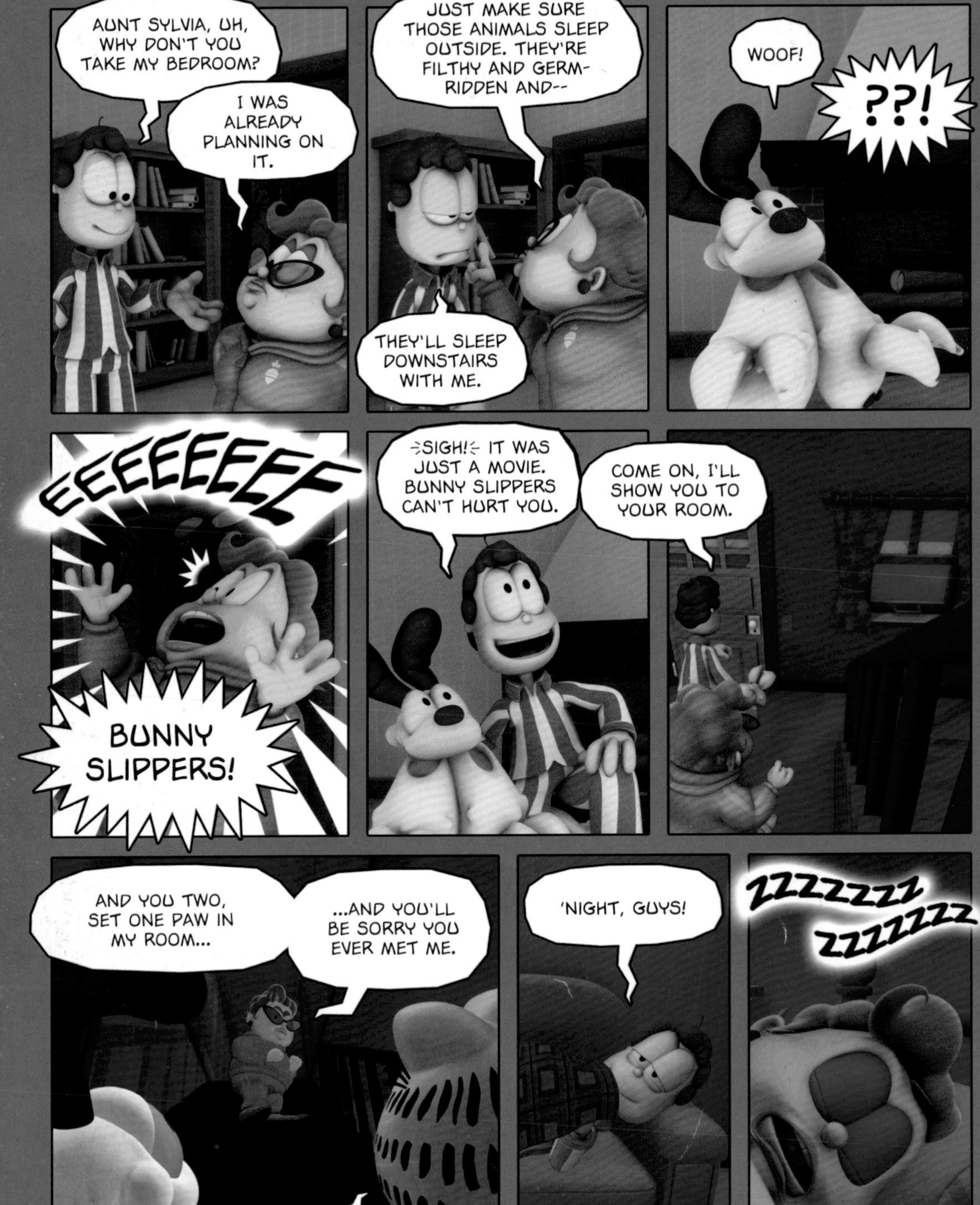
AUNT SYLVIA, UH, WHY DON'T YOU TAKE MY BEDROOM?
I WAS ALREADY PLANNING ON IT.
JUST MAKE SURE THOSE ANIMALS SLEEP OUTSIDE. THEY'RE FILTHY AND GERM-RIDDEN AND--
THEY'LL SLEEP DOWNSTAIRS WITH ME.
WOOF!
??!
EEEEEEEE
BUNNY SLIPPERS!
SIGH! IT WAS JUST A MOVIE. BUNNY SLIPPERS CAN'T HURT YOU.
COME ON, I'LL SHOW YOU TO YOUR ROOM.
AND YOU TWO, SET ONE PAW IN MY ROOM...
...AND YOU'LL BE SORRY YOU EVER MET ME.
IT'S A LITTLE LATE FOR THAT.
'NIGHT, GUYS!
ZZZZZZZ
ZZZZZZZ

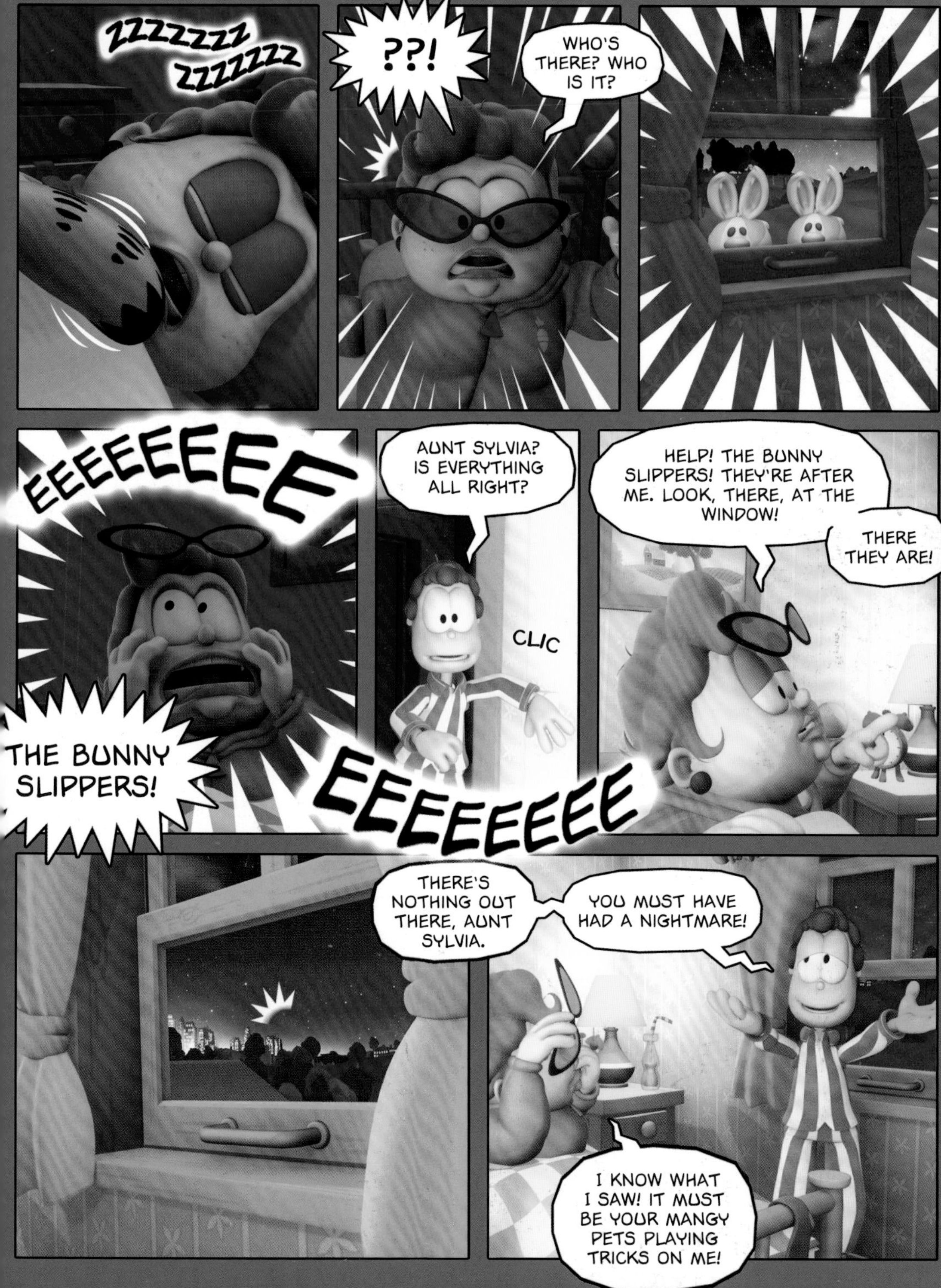
ZZZZZZZ
ZZZZZZZ
??!
WHO'S THERE? WHO IS IT?
EEEEEEEE
THE BUNNY SLIPPERS!
AUNT SYLVIA? IS EVERYTHING ALL RIGHT?
CLIC
EEEEEEEE
HELP! THE BUNNY SLIPPERS! THEY'RE AFTER ME. LOOK, THERE, AT THE WINDOW!
THERE THEY ARE!
THERE'S NOTHING OUT THERE, AUNT SYLVIA.
YOU MUST HAVE HAD A NIGHTMARE!
I KNOW WHAT I SAW! IT MUST BE YOUR MANGY PETS PLAYING TRICKS ON ME!

GARFIELD AND ODIE? DO YOU REALLY THINK THEY'D DO SOMETHING ROTTEN TO YOU?

'NIGHT, AUNT SYLVIA.

CLIC

I NEED TO GET SOME SLEEP. MAYBE THESE EAR-PLUGS WILL ⇒YAWN!⇐ MAKE THAT POSSIBLE.

ZZZZZZZ
ZZZZZZZ

HEH, HEH, HEH.

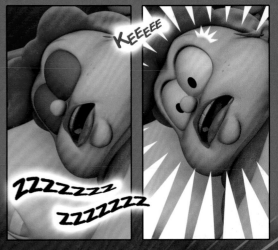

KEEEEE

ZZZZZZZ
ZZZZZZZ

KEEEEE

KEEEEE

??!

KEEEEE

BOING

BOING

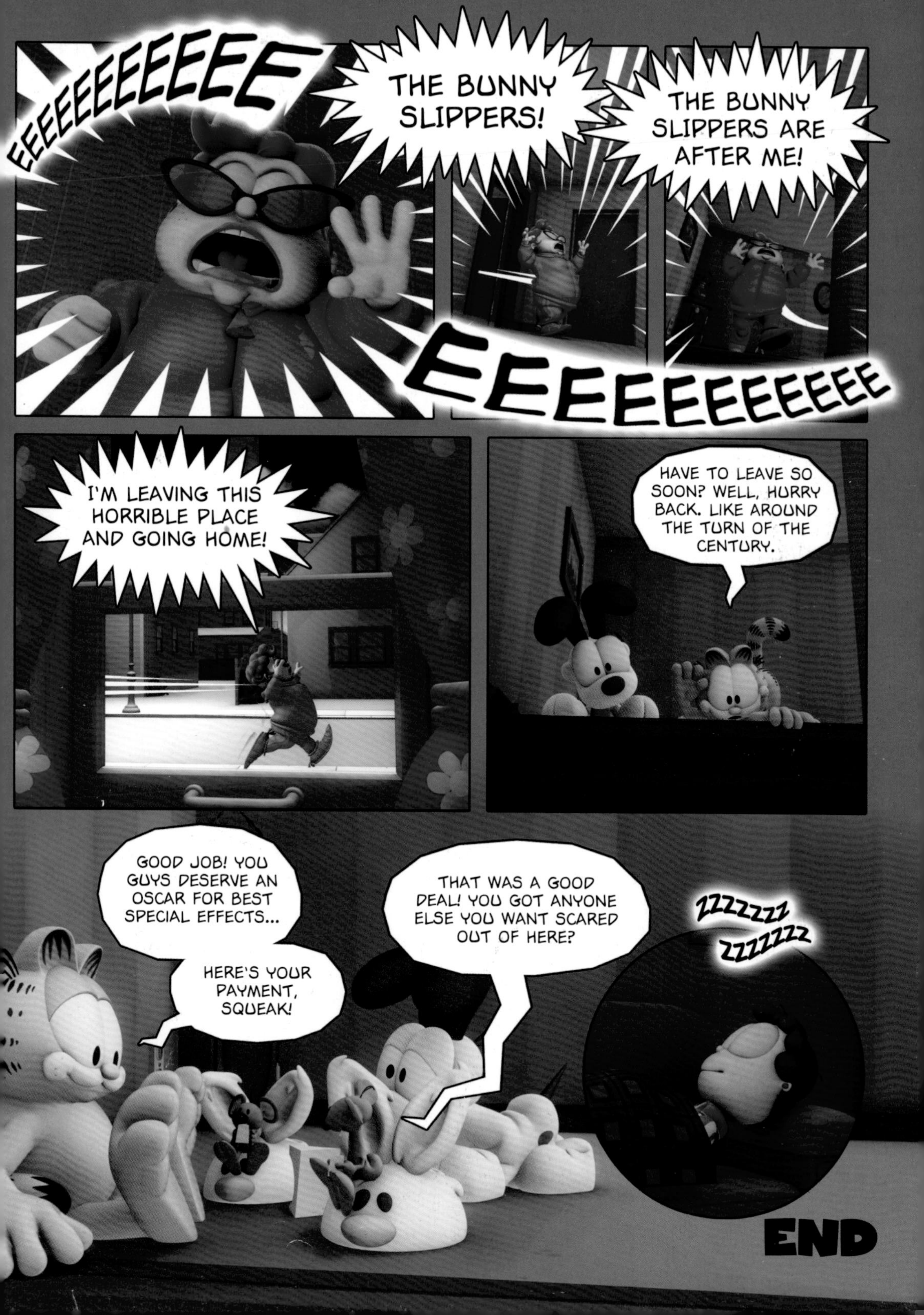
EEEEEEEEEEEE
THE BUNNY SLIPPERS!
THE BUNNY SLIPPERS ARE AFTER ME!
EEEEEEEEEEEE
I'M LEAVING THIS HORRIBLE PLACE AND GOING HOME!
HAVE TO LEAVE SO SOON? WELL, HURRY BACK. LIKE AROUND THE TURN OF THE CENTURY.
GOOD JOB! YOU GUYS DESERVE AN OSCAR FOR BEST SPECIAL EFFECTS...
HERE'S YOUR PAYMENT, SQUEAK!
THAT WAS A GOOD DEAL! YOU GOT ANYONE ELSE YOU WANT SCARED OUT OF HERE?
ZZZZZZZ
ZZZZZZZ
END

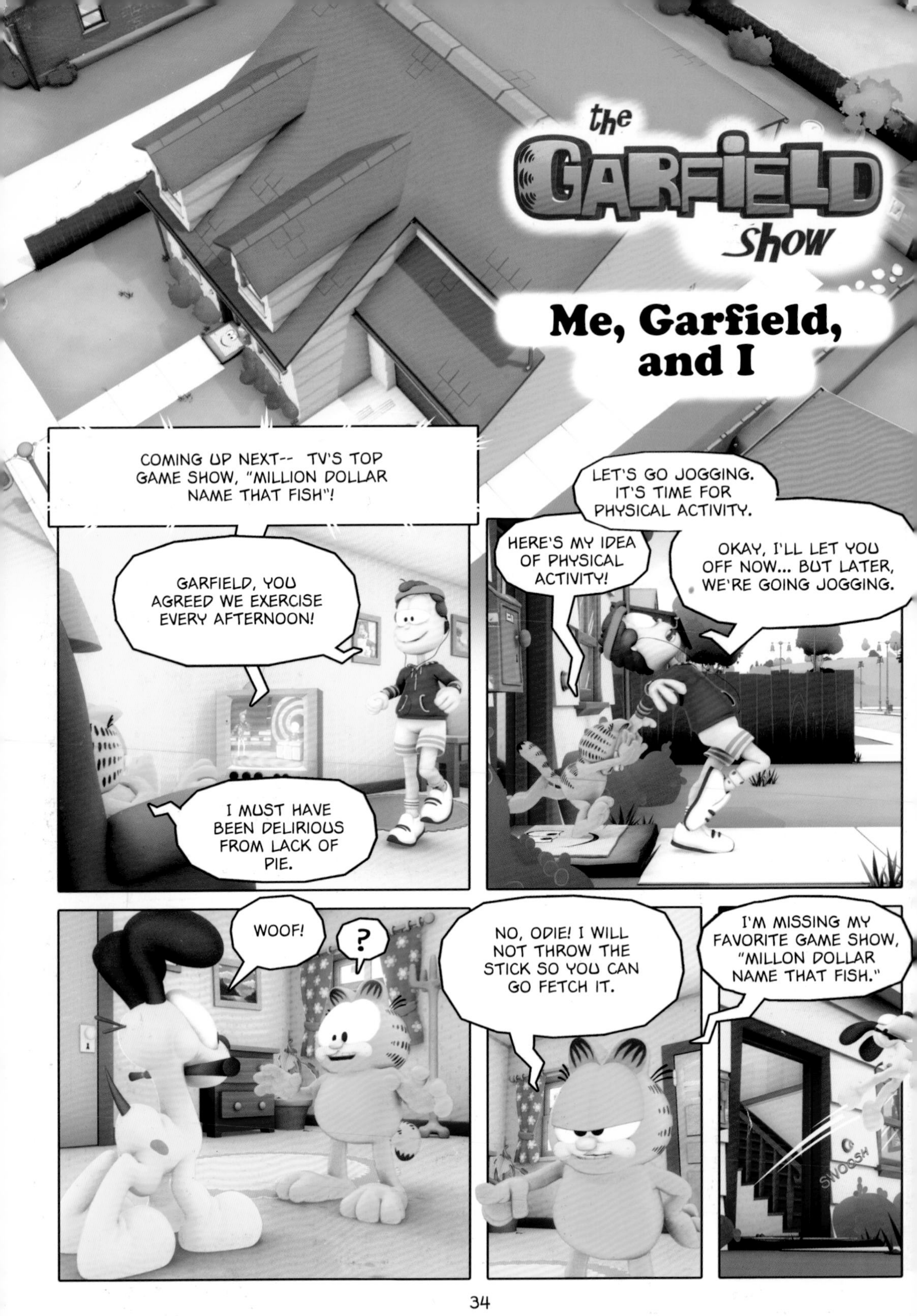
the GARFIELD Show
Me, Garfield, and I
COMING UP NEXT-- TV'S TOP GAME SHOW, "MILLION DOLLAR NAME THAT FISH"!
GARFIELD, YOU AGREED WE EXERCISE EVERY AFTERNOON!
I MUST HAVE BEEN DELIRIOUS FROM LACK OF PIE.
LET'S GO JOGGING. IT'S TIME FOR PHYSICAL ACTIVITY.
HERE'S MY IDEA OF PHYSICAL ACTIVITY!
OKAY, I'LL LET YOU OFF NOW... BUT LATER, WE'RE GOING JOGGING.
WOOF!
?
NO, ODIE! I WILL NOT THROW THE STICK SO YOU CAN GO FETCH IT.
I'M MISSING MY FAVORITE GAME SHOW, "MILLON DOLLAR NAME THAT FISH."
SWOOSH

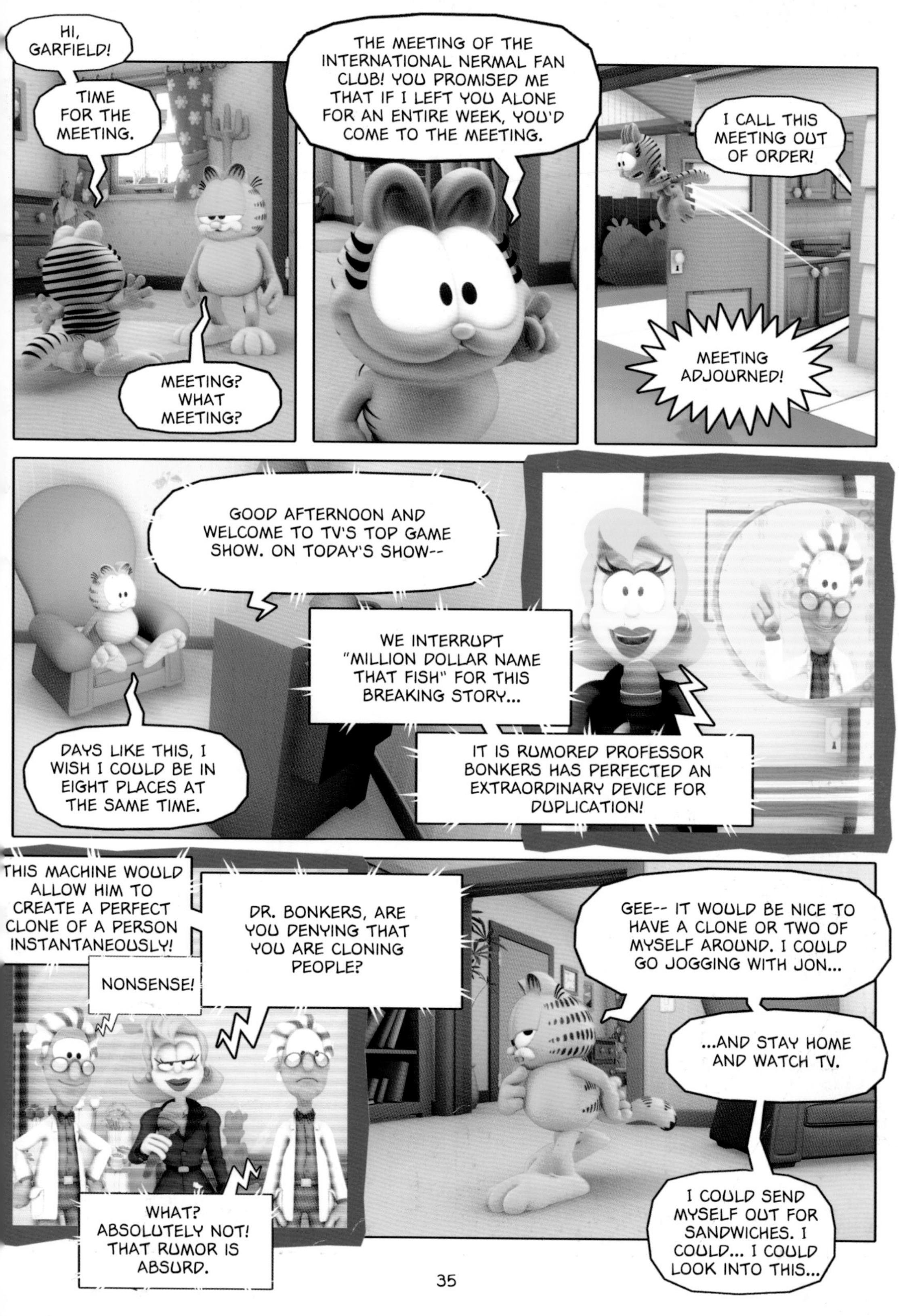
HI, GARFIELD!
TIME FOR THE MEETING.
MEETING? WHAT MEETING?
THE MEETING OF THE INTERNATIONAL NERMAL FAN CLUB! YOU PROMISED ME THAT IF I LEFT YOU ALONE FOR AN ENTIRE WEEK, YOU'D COME TO THE MEETING.
I CALL THIS MEETING OUT OF ORDER!
MEETING ADJOURNED!
GOOD AFTERNOON AND WELCOME TO TV'S TOP GAME SHOW. ON TODAY'S SHOW--
WE INTERRUPT "MILLION DOLLAR NAME THAT FISH" FOR THIS BREAKING STORY...
IT IS RUMORED PROFESSOR BONKERS HAS PERFECTED AN EXTRAORDINARY DEVICE FOR DUPLICATION!
DAYS LIKE THIS, I WISH I COULD BE IN EIGHT PLACES AT THE SAME TIME.
THIS MACHINE WOULD ALLOW HIM TO CREATE A PERFECT CLONE OF A PERSON INSTANTANEOUSLY!
NONSENSE!
DR. BONKERS, ARE YOU DENYING THAT YOU ARE CLONING PEOPLE?
WHAT? ABSOLUTELY NOT! THAT RUMOR IS ABSURD.
GEE-- IT WOULD BE NICE TO HAVE A CLONE OR TWO OF MYSELF AROUND. I COULD GO JOGGING WITH JON...
...AND STAY HOME AND WATCH TV.
I COULD SEND MYSELF OUT FOR SANDWICHES. I COULD... I COULD LOOK INTO THIS...

IF YOU ARE HERE TO ASK ABOUT MY CLONING RAY, PUSSYCAT, YOU'RE WASTING YOUR TIME!
I DO NOT WANT THE PUBLIC TO KNOW ABOUT IT UNTIL IT IS PERFECTED.
I HAVE TO GO.
KZZZZZT
INCREDIBLE!
THE MAD SCIENTISTS LEAGUE IS HAVING A BASEBALL GAME TONIGHT. I AM THE ENTIRE STARTING LINE-UP.
OH, MY... HE LEFT THE CLONING RAY OUT COMPLETELY UNGUARDED.
IT WOULD BE WRONG OF ME TO BORROW IT, TAKE IT HOME, AND MAKE DUPLICATES OF MYSELF.
IF ANYONE ASKS, TELL THEM MY EVIL CLONE TOOK IT.

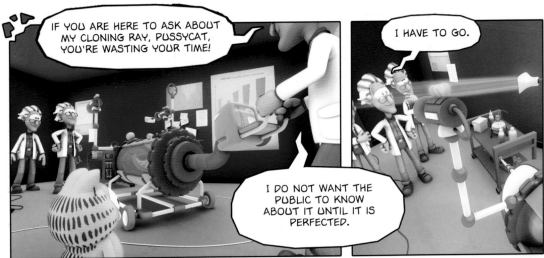

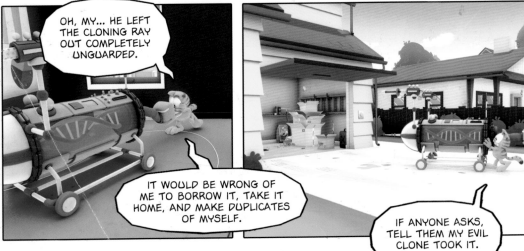

NO EXCUSES THIS TIME. WE'RE GOING JOGGING-- NOW!

SURE. JUST GIVE ME A SECOND...

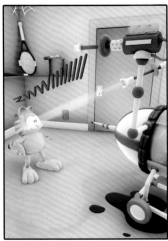

ZWWW

ZZZZ-T

READY TO GET SOME EXERCISE?

SINCE THIS IS YOUR FIRST RUN, WE'LL ONLY DO 15 MILES AND HEAD HOME.

WHILE THEY'RE GETTING ALL SWEATY--

--MAYBE I CAN FINALLY WATCH SOME TV!

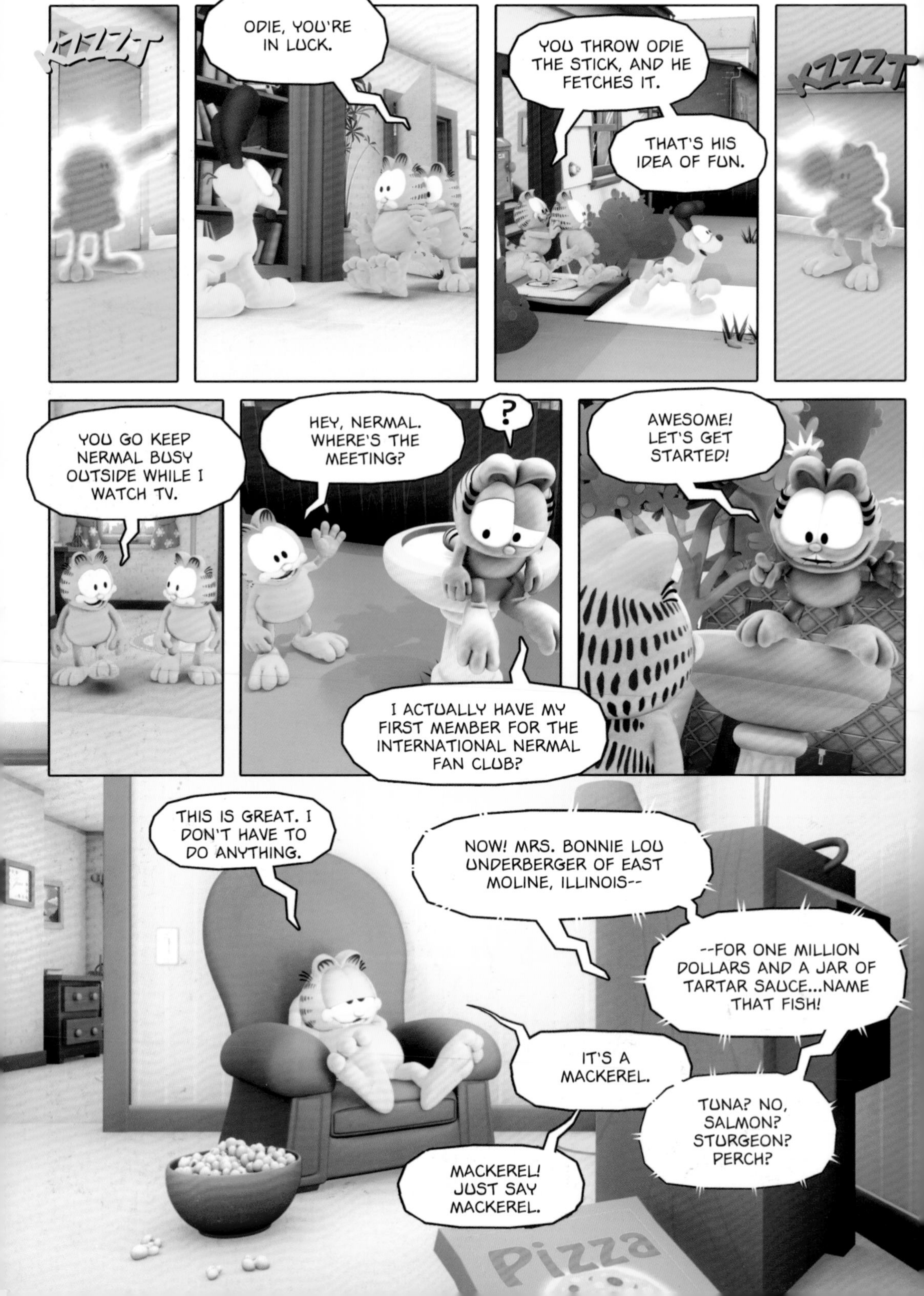
KZZZ-T
ODIE, YOU'RE IN LUCK.
YOU THROW ODIE THE STICK, AND HE FETCHES IT.
THAT'S HIS IDEA OF FUN.
KZZZT
YOU GO KEEP NERMAL BUSY OUTSIDE WHILE I WATCH TV.
HEY, NERMAL. WHERE'S THE MEETING?
?
I ACTUALLY HAVE MY FIRST MEMBER FOR THE INTERNATIONAL NERMAL FAN CLUB?
AWESOME! LET'S GET STARTED!
THIS IS GREAT. I DON'T HAVE TO DO ANYTHING.
NOW! MRS. BONNIE LOU UNDERBERGER OF EAST MOLINE, ILLINOIS--
--FOR ONE MILLION DOLLARS AND A JAR OF TARTAR SAUCE...NAME THAT FISH!
IT'S A MACKEREL.
TUNA? NO, SALMON? STURGEON? PERCH?
MACKEREL! JUST SAY MACKEREL.
Pizza

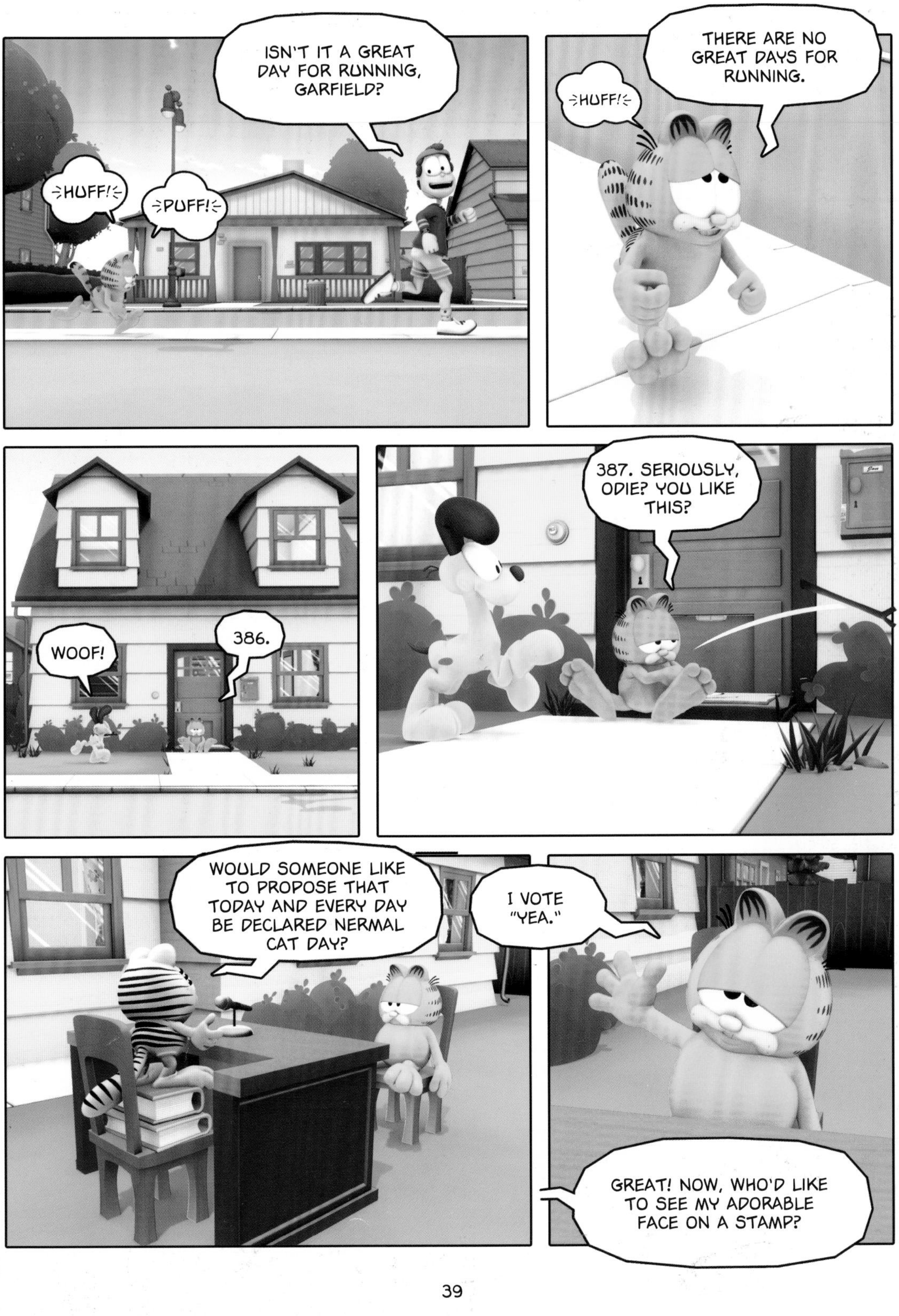
ISN'T IT A GREAT DAY FOR RUNNING, GARFIELD?
HUFF!
PUFF!
HUFF!
THERE ARE NO GREAT DAYS FOR RUNNING.
WOOF!
386.
387. SERIOUSLY, ODIE? YOU LIKE THIS?
WOULD SOMEONE LIKE TO PROPOSE THAT TODAY AND EVERY DAY BE DECLARED NERMAL CAT DAY?
I VOTE "YEA."
GREAT! NOW, WHO'D LIKE TO SEE MY ADORABLE FACE ON A STAMP?

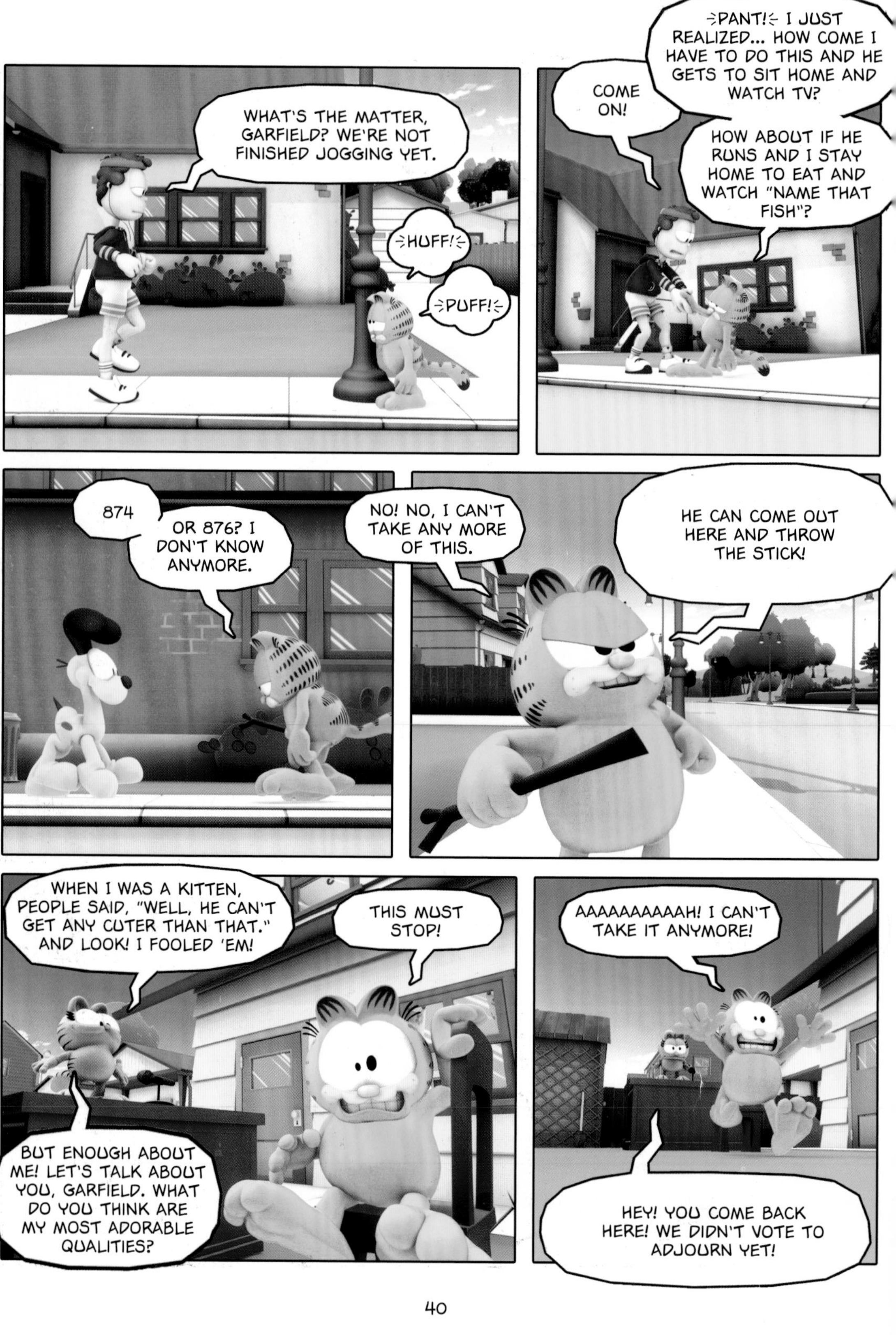
WHAT'S THE MATTER, GARFIELD? WE'RE NOT FINISHED JOGGING YET.
HUFF!
PUFF!
COME ON!
PANT! I JUST REALIZED... HOW COME I HAVE TO DO THIS AND HE GETS TO SIT HOME AND WATCH TV?
HOW ABOUT IF HE RUNS AND I STAY HOME TO EAT AND WATCH "NAME THAT FISH"?
874
OR 876? I DON'T KNOW ANYMORE.
NO! NO, I CAN'T TAKE ANY MORE OF THIS.
HE CAN COME OUT HERE AND THROW THE STICK!
WHEN I WAS A KITTEN, PEOPLE SAID, "WELL, HE CAN'T GET ANY CUTER THAN THAT." AND LOOK! I FOOLED 'EM!
BUT ENOUGH ABOUT ME! LET'S TALK ABOUT YOU, GARFIELD. WHAT DO YOU THINK ARE MY MOST ADORABLE QUALITIES?
THIS MUST STOP!
AAAAAAAAAAH! I CAN'T TAKE IT ANYMORE!
HEY! YOU COME BACK HERE! WE DIDN'T VOTE TO ADJOURN YET!

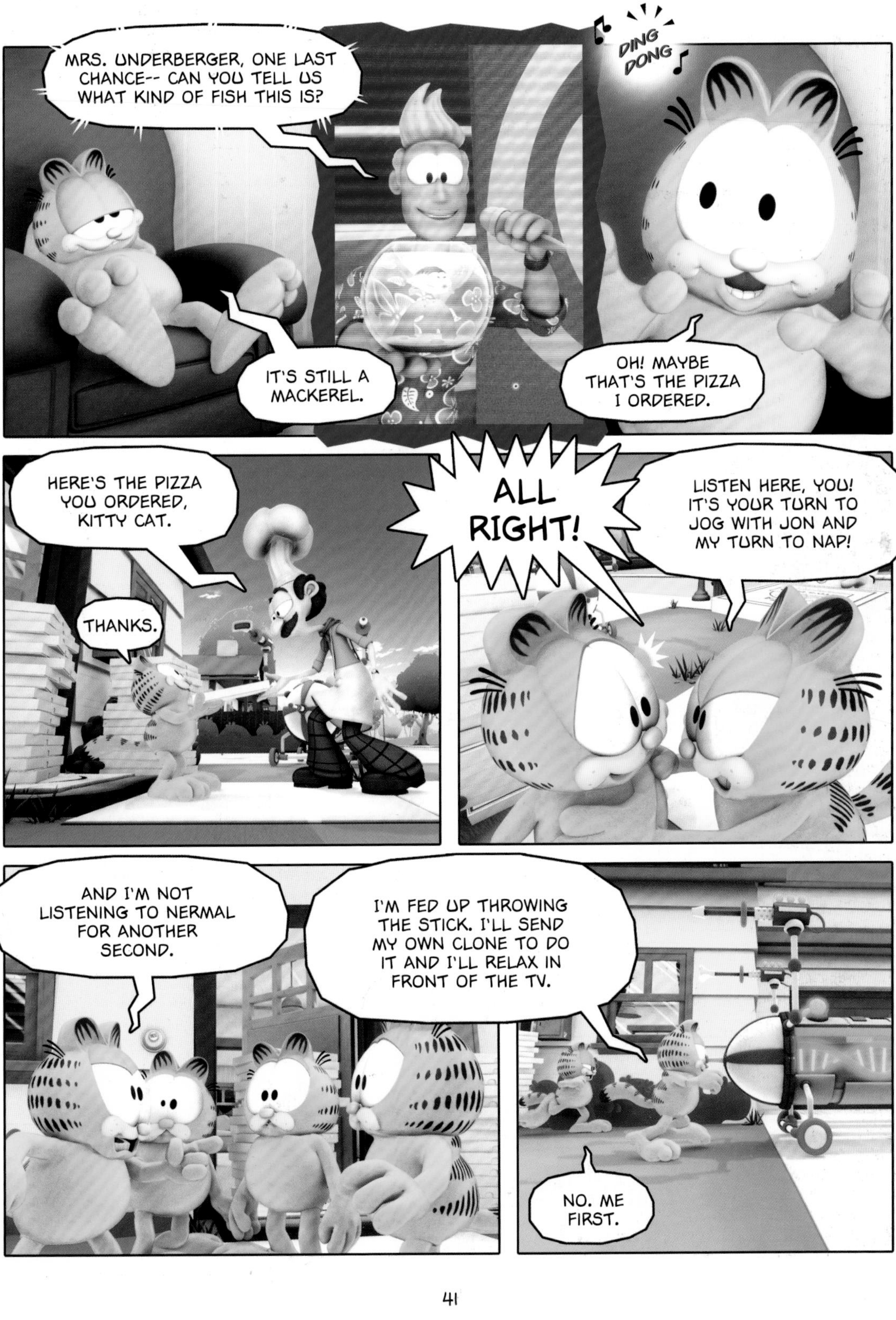

DING DONG
MRS. UNDERBERGER, ONE LAST CHANCE-- CAN YOU TELL US WHAT KIND OF FISH THIS IS?
IT'S STILL A MACKEREL.
OH! MAYBE THAT'S THE PIZZA I ORDERED.
HERE'S THE PIZZA YOU ORDERED, KITTY CAT.
THANKS.
ALL RIGHT!
LISTEN HERE, YOU! IT'S YOUR TURN TO JOG WITH JON AND MY TURN TO NAP!
AND I'M NOT LISTENING TO NERMAL FOR ANOTHER SECOND.
I'M FED UP THROWING THE STICK. I'LL SEND MY OWN CLONE TO DO IT AND I'LL RELAX IN FRONT OF THE TV.
NO. ME FIRST.

I'M GOING TO MAKE MY CLONE.

NO, I AM!

STOP! YOU'LL BREAK THE MACHINE!

?!

BZZZZT

BLAF

ZWIIII

?

ZWIIII

ZWIIII

ZWIIII

ZWIIII

ZWIIII

?

K-ZZZT

KZZZT

KZZZT

WHAT'S GOING ON HERE?

STOP! EVERYONE, STOP.

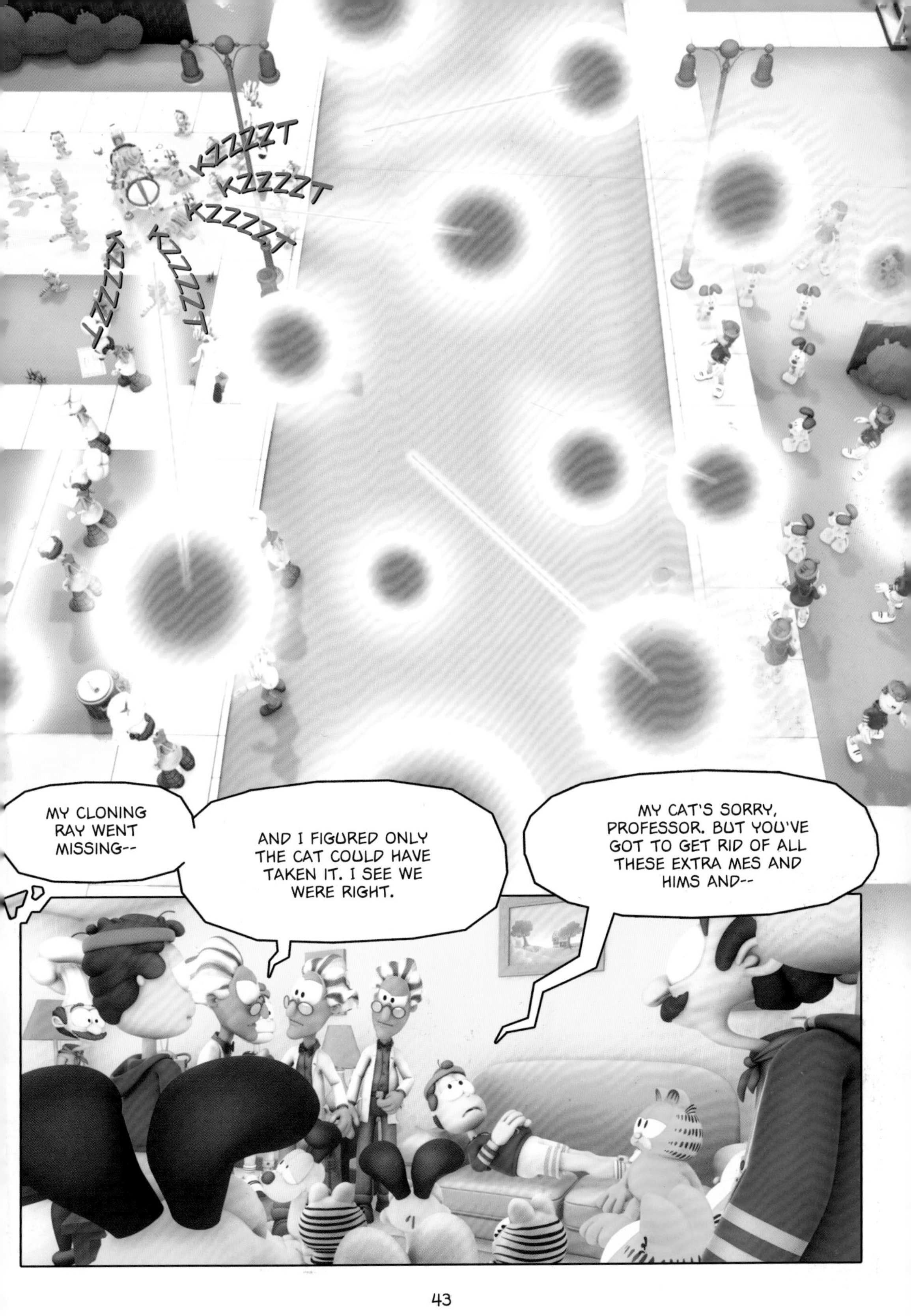
KZZZZT
KZZZZZT
KZZZZZT
KZZZZZT
KZZZZZT
MY CLONING RAY WENT MISSING--
AND I FIGURED ONLY THE CAT COULD HAVE TAKEN IT. I SEE WE WERE RIGHT.
MY CAT'S SORRY, PROFESSOR. BUT YOU'VE GOT TO GET RID OF ALL THESE EXTRA MES AND HIMS AND--

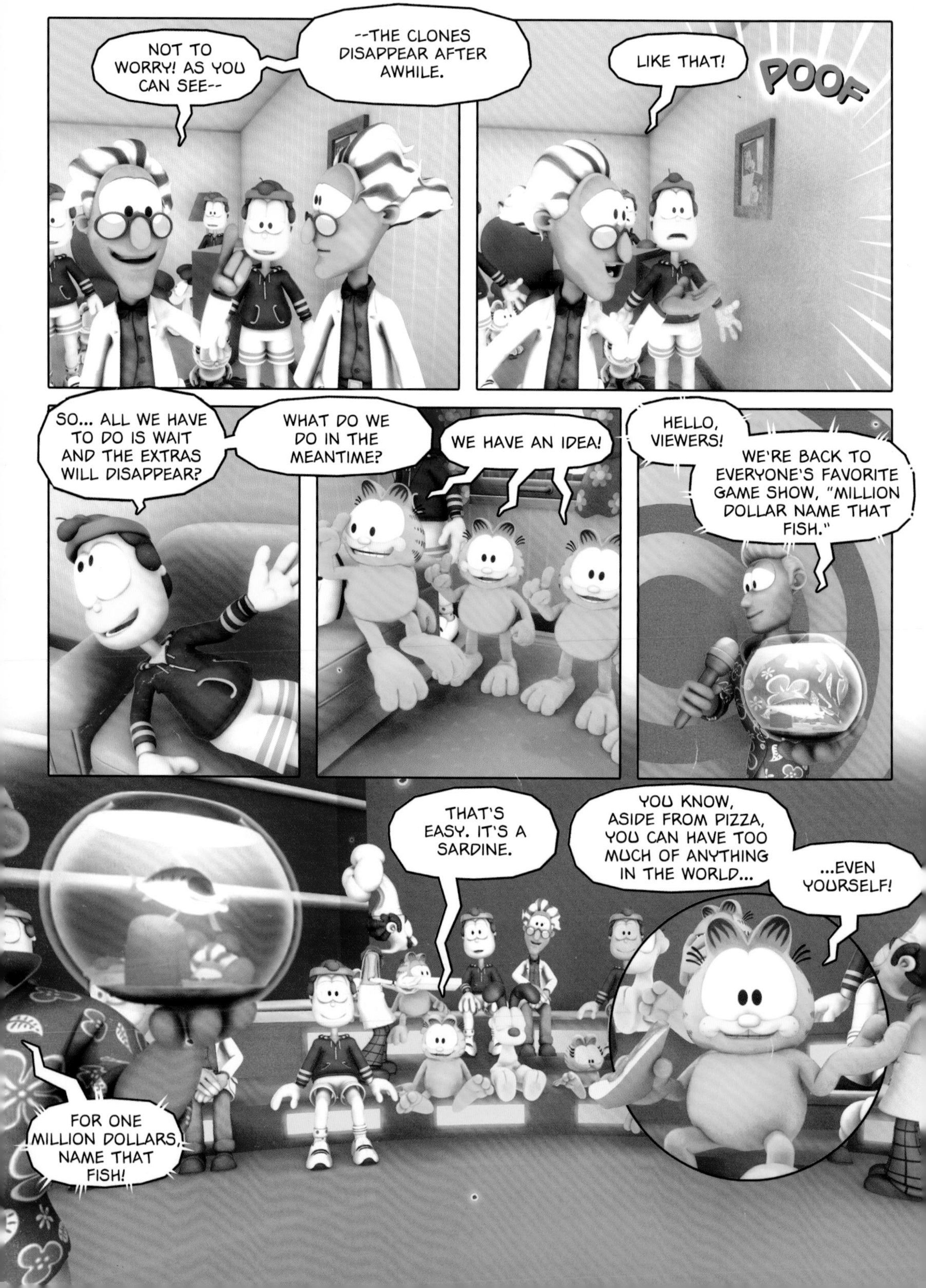
NOT TO WORRY! AS YOU CAN SEE--
--THE CLONES DISAPPEAR AFTER AWHILE.
LIKE THAT!
POOF
SO... ALL WE HAVE TO DO IS WAIT AND THE EXTRAS WILL DISAPPEAR?
WHAT DO WE DO IN THE MEANTIME?
WE HAVE AN IDEA!
HELLO, VIEWERS!
WE'RE BACK TO EVERYONE'S FAVORITE GAME SHOW, "MILLION DOLLAR NAME THAT FISH."
FOR ONE MILLION DOLLARS, NAME THAT FISH!
THAT'S EASY. IT'S A SARDINE.
YOU KNOW, ASIDE FROM PIZZA, YOU CAN HAVE TOO MUCH OF ANYTHING IN THE WORLD...
...EVEN YOURSELF!

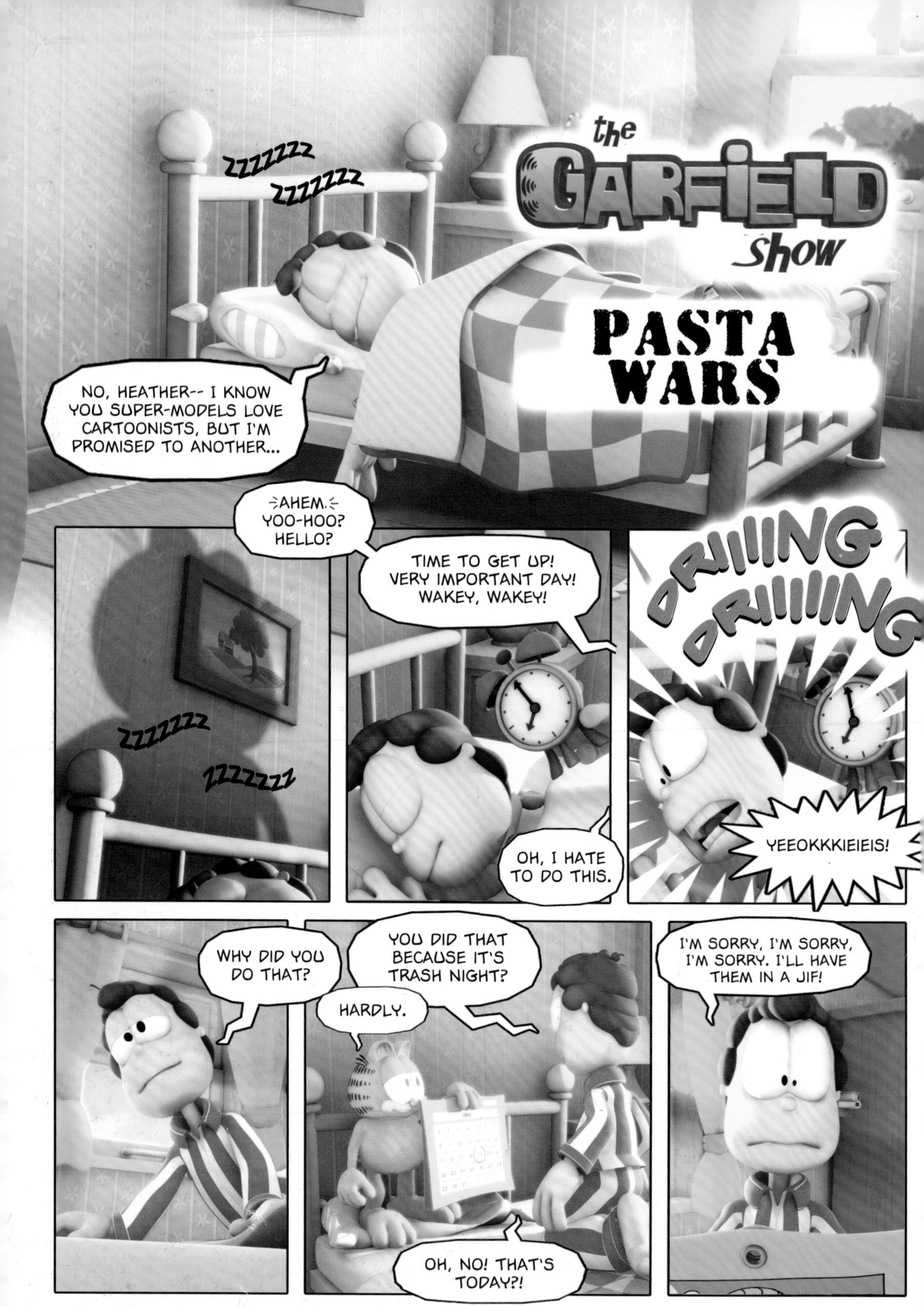

the GARFIELD show
PASTA WARS
ZZZZZZZ
ZZZZZZZ
NO, HEATHER-- I KNOW YOU SUPER-MODELS LOVE CARTOONISTS, BUT I'M PROMISED TO ANOTHER...
AHEM. YOO-HOO? HELLO?
ZZZZZZZ
ZZZZZZZ
TIME TO GET UP! VERY IMPORTANT DAY! WAKEY, WAKEY!
OH, I HATE TO DO THIS.
DRIIIING DRIIIING
YEEOKKKIEIEIS!
WHY DID YOU DO THAT?
YOU DID THAT BECAUSE IT'S TRASH NIGHT?
HARDLY.
OH, NO! THAT'S TODAY?!
I'M SORRY, I'M SORRY, I'M SORRY. I'LL HAVE THEM IN A JIF!

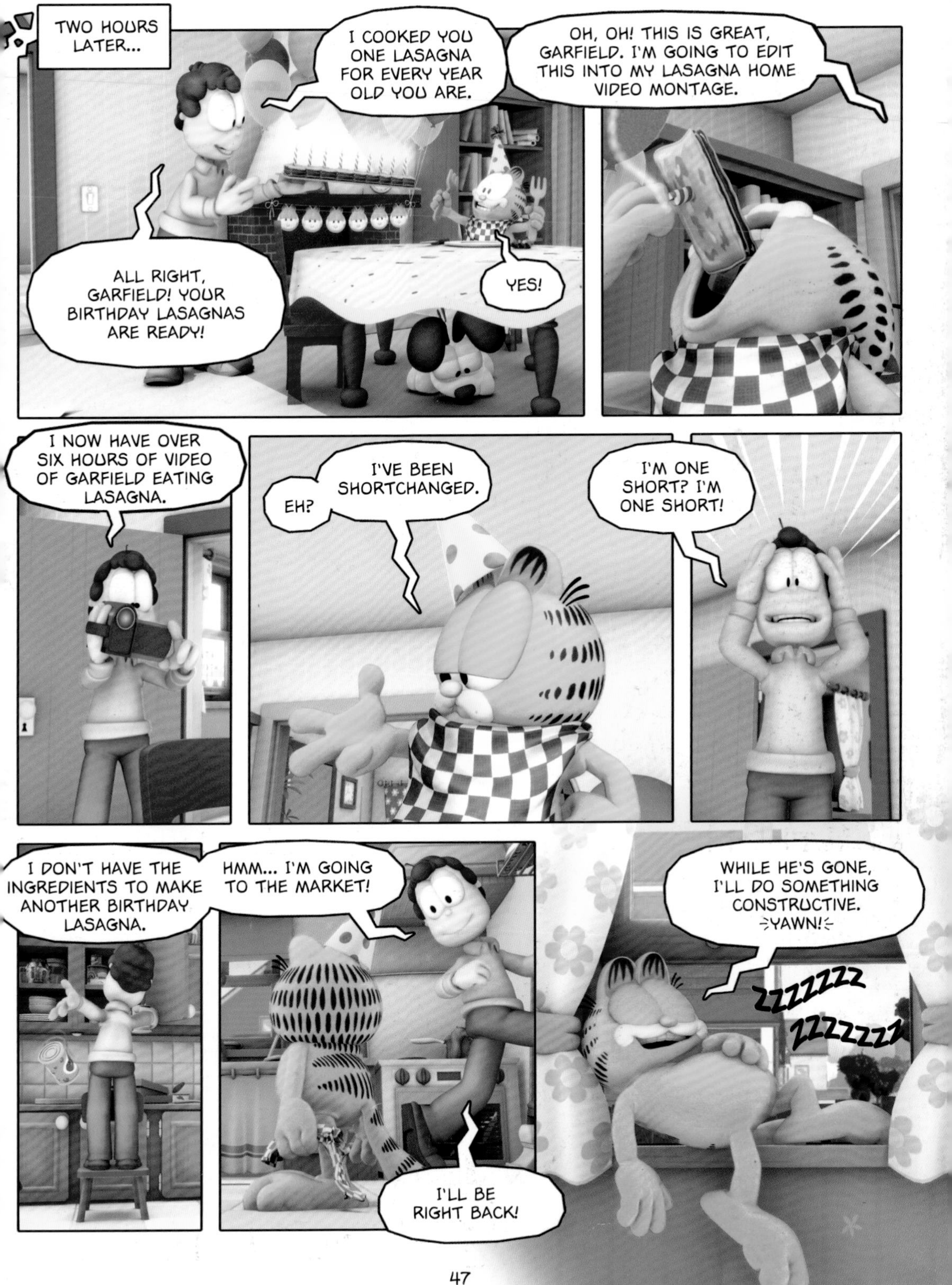
TWO HOURS LATER...
I COOKED YOU ONE LASAGNA FOR EVERY YEAR OLD YOU ARE.
ALL RIGHT, GARFIELD! YOUR BIRTHDAY LASAGNAS ARE READY!
YES!
OH, OH! THIS IS GREAT, GARFIELD. I'M GOING TO EDIT THIS INTO MY LASAGNA HOME VIDEO MONTAGE.
I NOW HAVE OVER SIX HOURS OF VIDEO OF GARFIELD EATING LASAGNA.
I'VE BEEN SHORTCHANGED.
EH?
I'M ONE SHORT? I'M ONE SHORT!
I DON'T HAVE THE INGREDIENTS TO MAKE ANOTHER BIRTHDAY LASAGNA.
HMM... I'M GOING TO THE MARKET!
I'LL BE RIGHT BACK!
WHILE HE'S GONE, I'LL DO SOMETHING CONSTRUCTIVE.
YAWN!
ZZZZZZZ
ZZZZZZZ

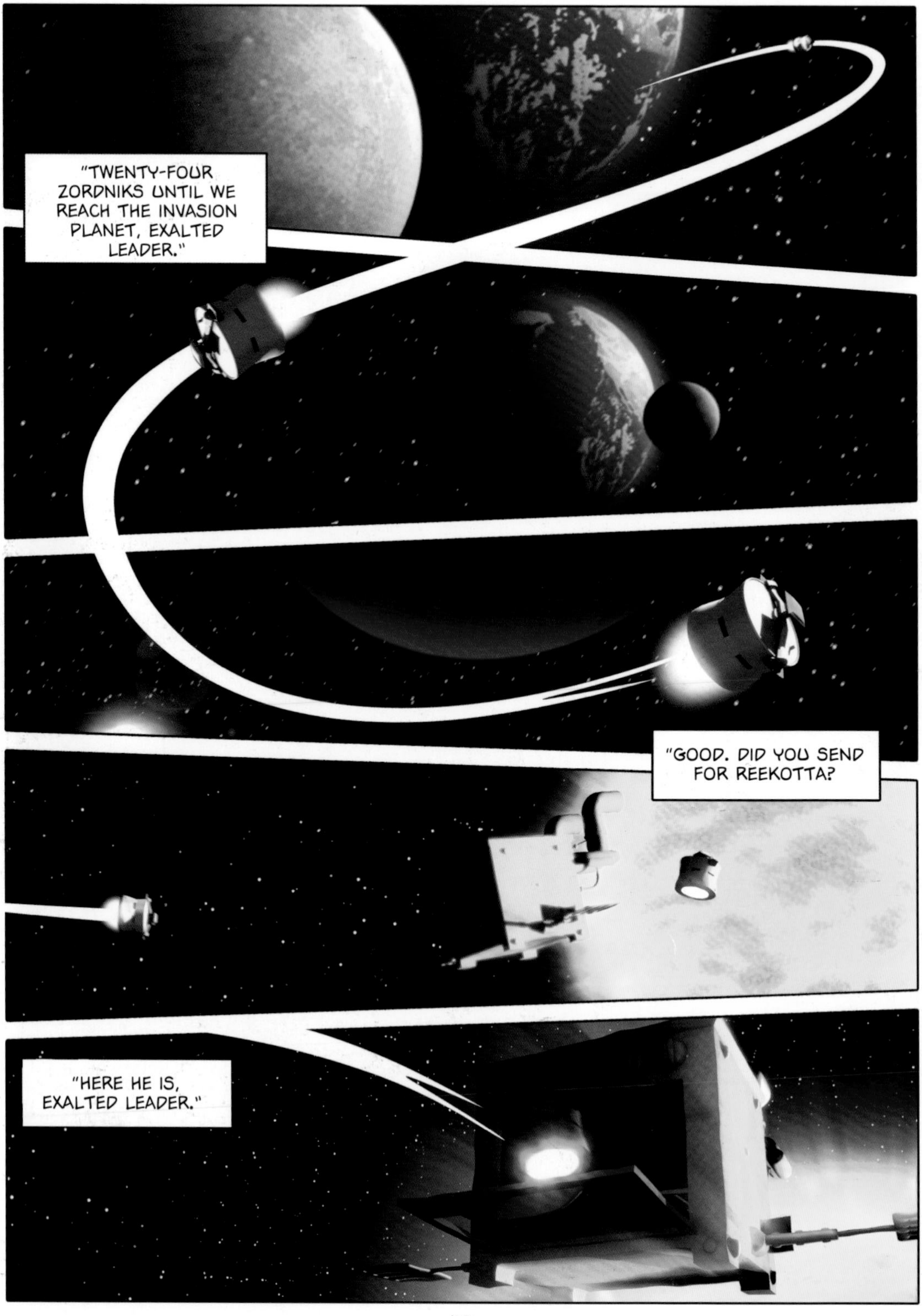
"TWENTY-FOUR ZORDNIKS UNTIL WE REACH THE INVASION PLANET, EXALTED LEADER."
"GOOD. DID YOU SEND FOR REEKOTTA?
"HERE HE IS, EXALTED LEADER."

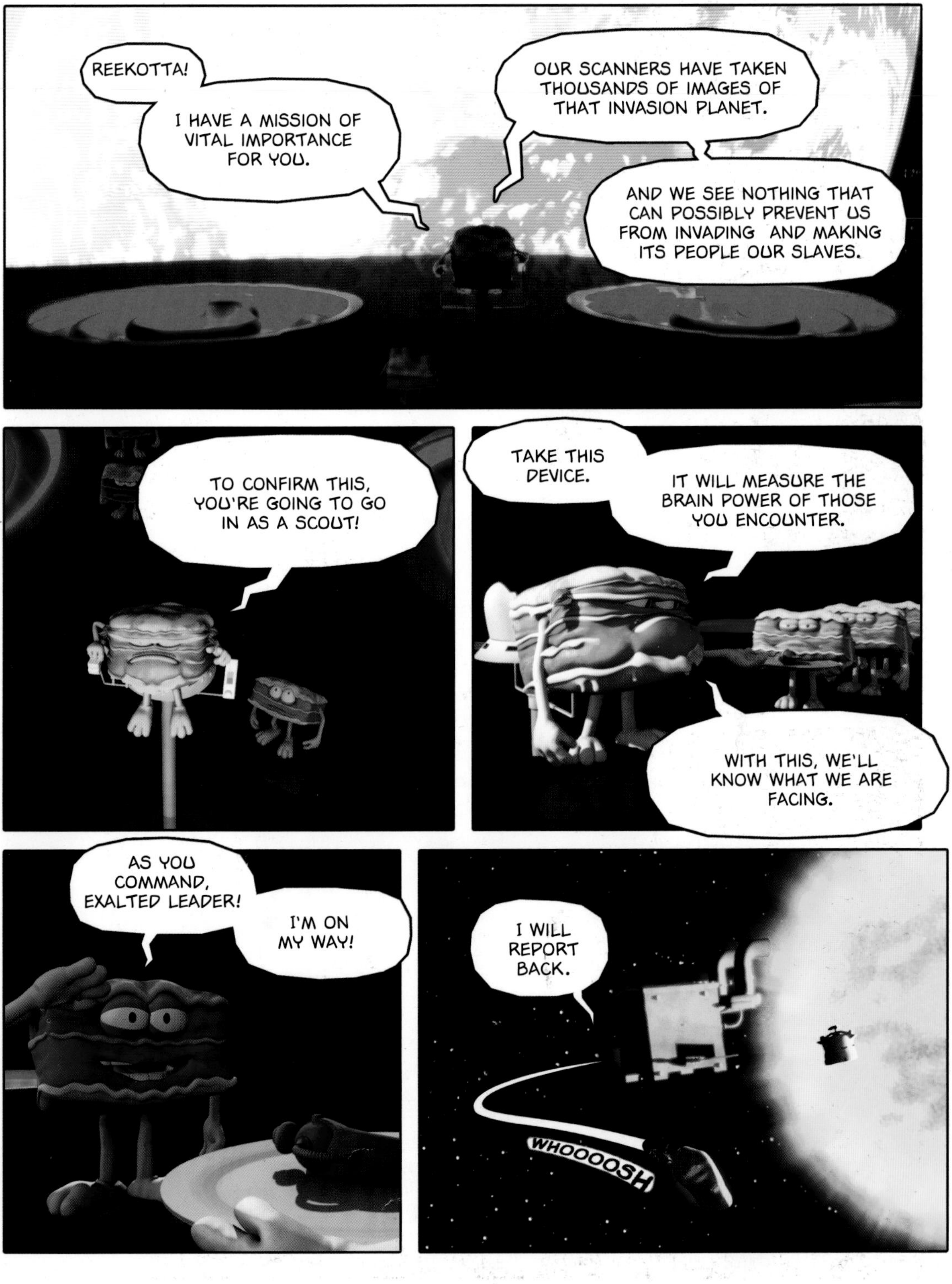
REEKOTTA!
I HAVE A MISSION OF VITAL IMPORTANCE FOR YOU.
OUR SCANNERS HAVE TAKEN THOUSANDS OF IMAGES OF THAT INVASION PLANET.
AND WE SEE NOTHING THAT CAN POSSIBLY PREVENT US FROM INVADING AND MAKING ITS PEOPLE OUR SLAVES.
TO CONFIRM THIS, YOU'RE GOING TO GO IN AS A SCOUT!
TAKE THIS DEVICE.
IT WILL MEASURE THE BRAIN POWER OF THOSE YOU ENCOUNTER.
WITH THIS, WE'LL KNOW WHAT WE ARE FACING.
AS YOU COMMAND, EXALTED LEADER!
I'M ON MY WAY!
I WILL REPORT BACK.
WHOOOOOSH

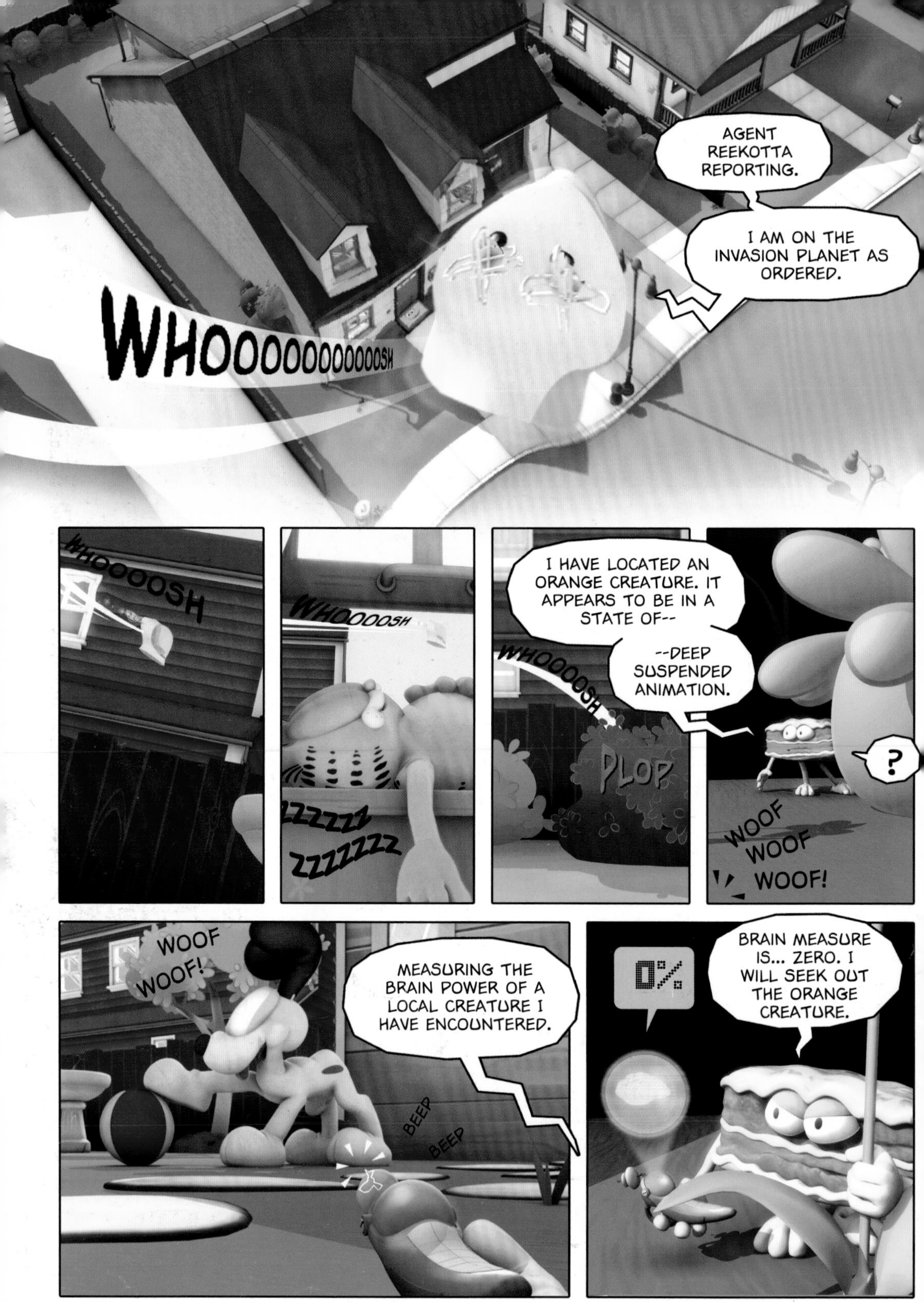
WHOOOOOOOOOOOSH
AGENT REEKOTTA REPORTING.
I AM ON THE INVASION PLANET AS ORDERED.
WHOOOOOSH
WHOOOOOSH
ZZZZZZ
ZZZZZZZ
I HAVE LOCATED AN ORANGE CREATURE. IT APPEARS TO BE IN A STATE OF--
WHOOOOOSH
--DEEP SUSPENDED ANIMATION.
PLOP
?
WOOF
WOOF
WOOF!
WOOF
WOOF!
MEASURING THE BRAIN POWER OF A LOCAL CREATURE I HAVE ENCOUNTERED.
BEEP
BEEP
0%
BRAIN MEASURE IS... ZERO. I WILL SEEK OUT THE ORANGE CREATURE.

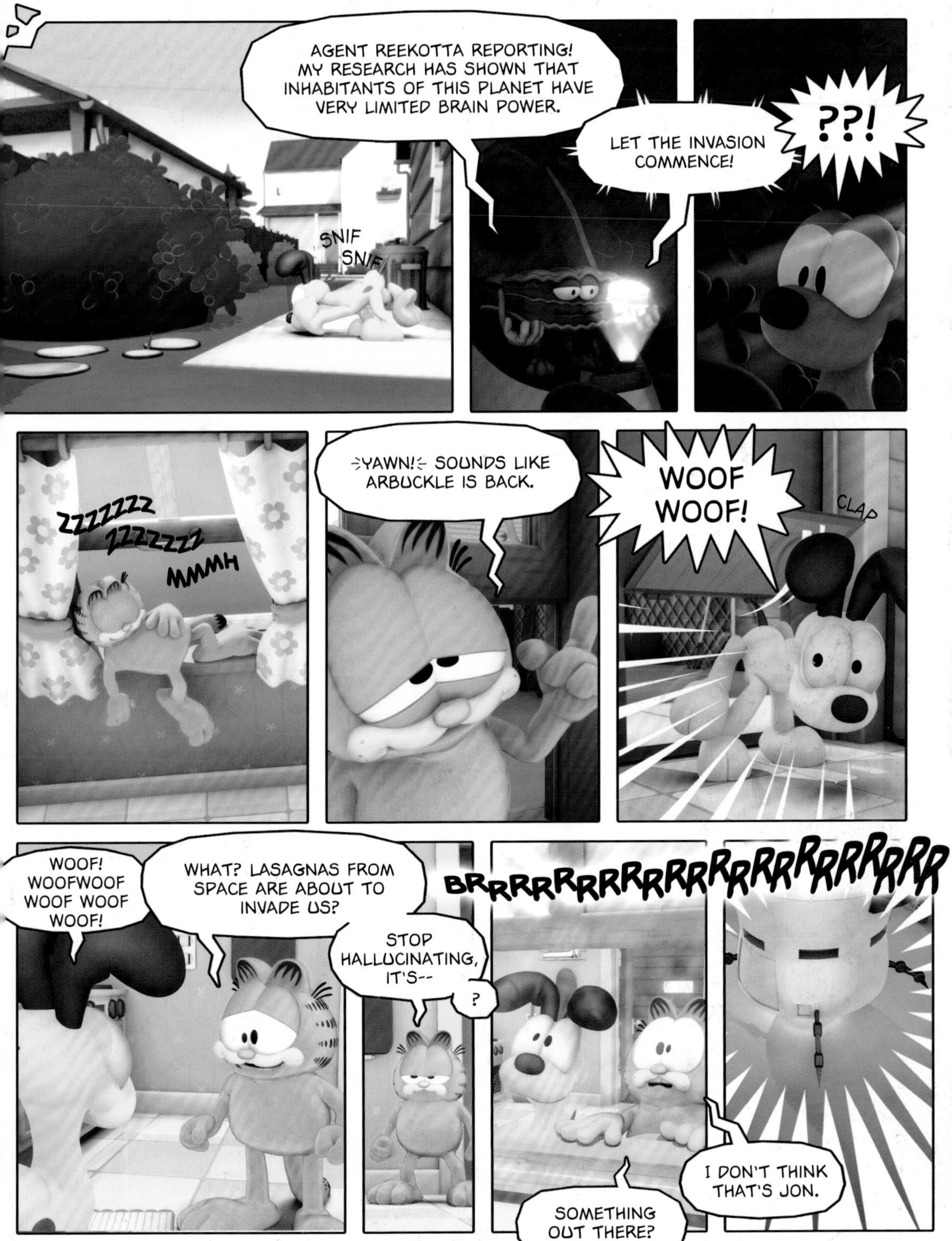
AGENT REEKOTTA REPORTING! MY RESEARCH HAS SHOWN THAT INHABITANTS OF THIS PLANET HAVE VERY LIMITED BRAIN POWER.
SNIF SNIF
LET THE INVASION COMMENCE!
??!
ZZZZZZZ ZZZZZZZ
MMMH
-YAWN!- SOUNDS LIKE ARBUCKLE IS BACK.
WOOF WOOF!
CLAP
WOOF! WOOFWOOF WOOF WOOF WOOF!
WHAT? LASAGNAS FROM SPACE ARE ABOUT TO INVADE US?
STOP HALLUCINATING, IT'S--
?
BRRRRRRRRRRRRRRRRRRRRRRR
SOMETHING OUT THERE?
I DON'T THINK THAT'S JON.

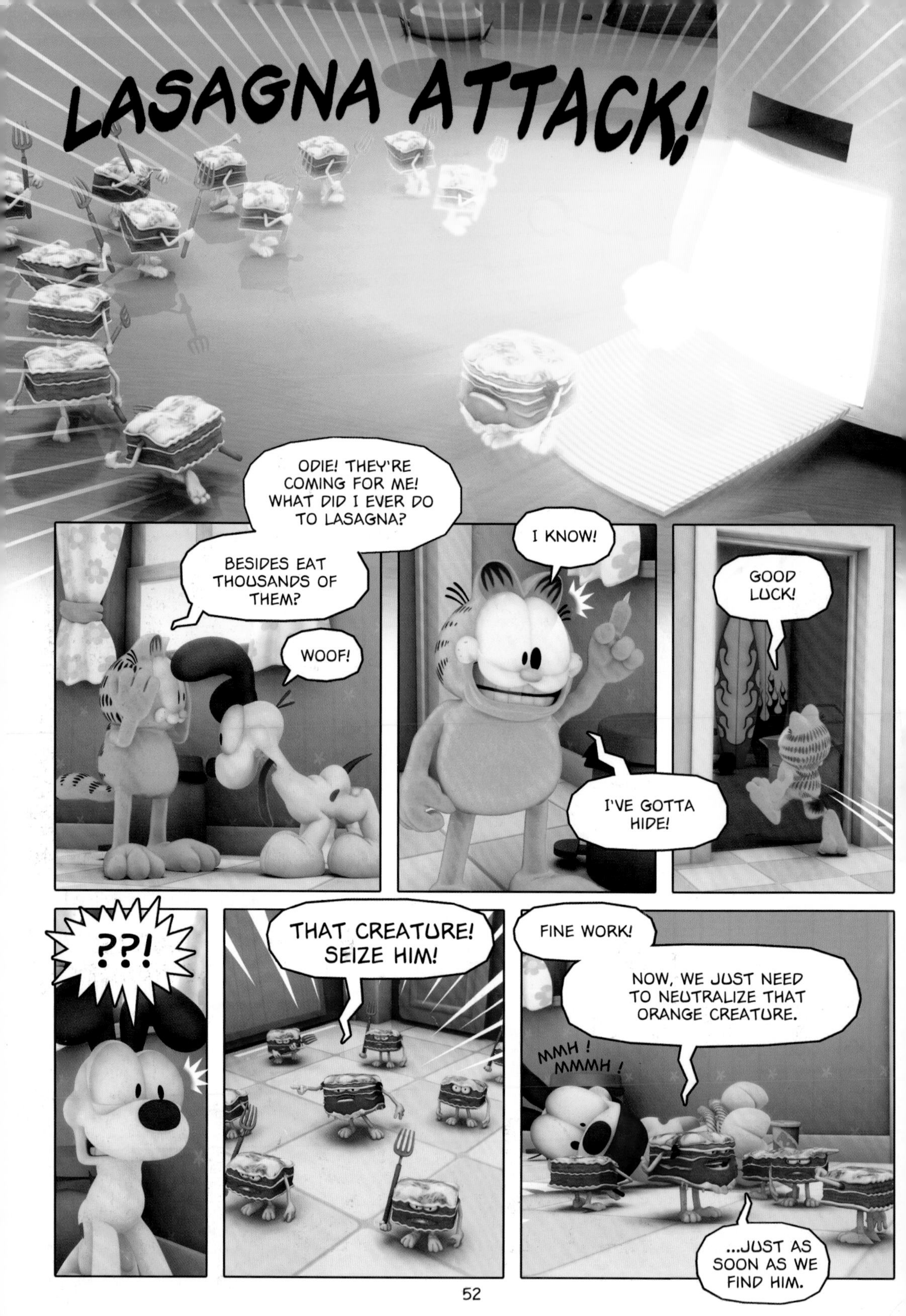

LASAGNA ATTACK!
ODIE! THEY'RE COMING FOR ME! WHAT DID I EVER DO TO LASAGNA?
BESIDES EAT THOUSANDS OF THEM?
WOOF!
I KNOW!
I'VE GOTTA HIDE!
GOOD LUCK!
??!
THAT CREATURE! SEIZE HIM!
FINE WORK!
NOW, WE JUST NEED TO NEUTRALIZE THAT ORANGE CREATURE.
MMH ! MMMH !
...JUST AS SOON AS WE FIND HIM.

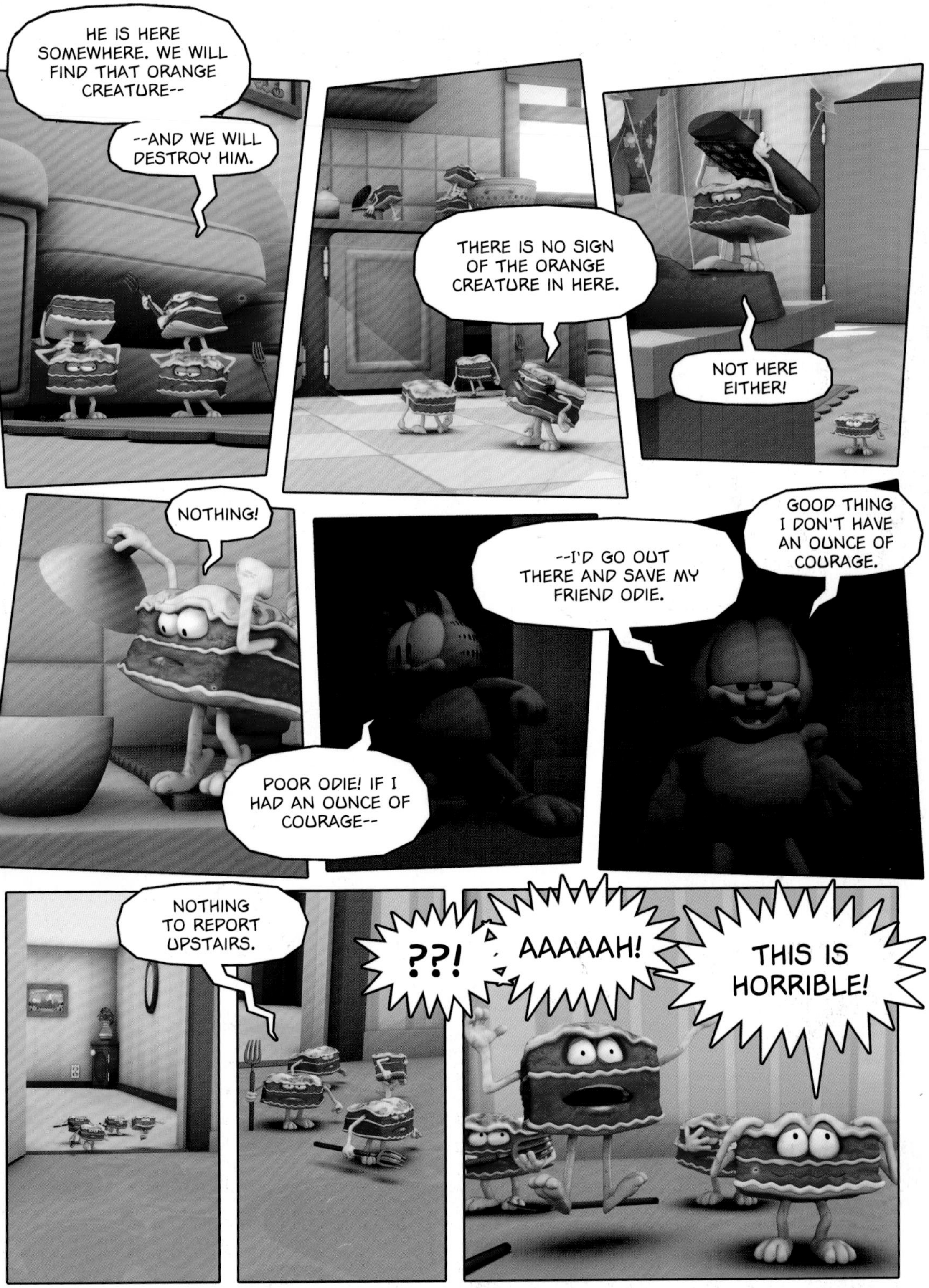

HE IS HERE SOMEWHERE. WE WILL FIND THAT ORANGE CREATURE--
--AND WE WILL DESTROY HIM.
THERE IS NO SIGN OF THE ORANGE CREATURE IN HERE.
NOT HERE EITHER!
NOTHING!
POOR ODIE! IF I HAD AN OUNCE OF COURAGE--
--I'D GO OUT THERE AND SAVE MY FRIEND ODIE.
GOOD THING I DON'T HAVE AN OUNCE OF COURAGE.
NOTHING TO REPORT UPSTAIRS.
??!
AAAAAH!
THIS IS HORRIBLE!

THIS IS SILLY. I CAN'T JUST HIDE IN HERE FOR THE REST OF MY LIFE... YES, I CAN. NO, I CAN'T.

JON? ODIE? TALKING LASAGNA?

MMH! MMMH!

LET'S UNTIE YOU.

THWIP

ODIE!

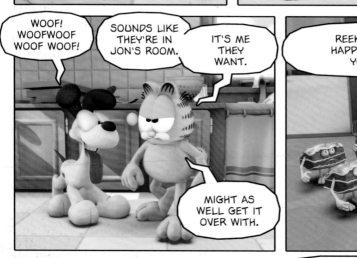

WOOF! WOOFWOOF WOOF WOOF!

SOUNDS LIKE THEY'RE IN JON'S ROOM.

IT'S ME THEY WANT.

MIGHT AS WELL GET IT OVER WITH.

REEKOTTA, WHAT'S HAPPENING? I HEARD YOU SCREAM!

EXALTED LEADER, IT'S--

--IT'S TERRIBLE, LOOK AT THE SCREEN!

THE HUMANITY!

÷GASP!÷ ÷CHOKE!÷

WE'RE IN THE HOME OF A MONSTER! YOU SEE HOW HE'S DEVOURING OUR BRETHREN!

IT'S DISGUSTING!

MM-MM!

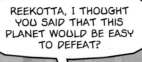

THEN AGAIN, I COULD JUST WAIT TILL JON COMES BACK...

REEKOTTA, I THOUGHT YOU SAID THAT THIS PLANET WOULD BE EASY TO DEFEAT?

I THOUGHT IT WOULD BE, BUT I HADN'T SEEN THAT CREATURE, EXALTED LEADER!

SOUNDS LIKE THEY'RE AFRAID OF ME...

GRRRRR

GUYS, IT'S TIME TO END THIS...

AAAAAA!

RUN AWAY!

IT'S THE MONSTER!

LET'S FLEE THIS PLANET!

BRRRRRRRRRRRRRRRRRRRRRRRRRRR!

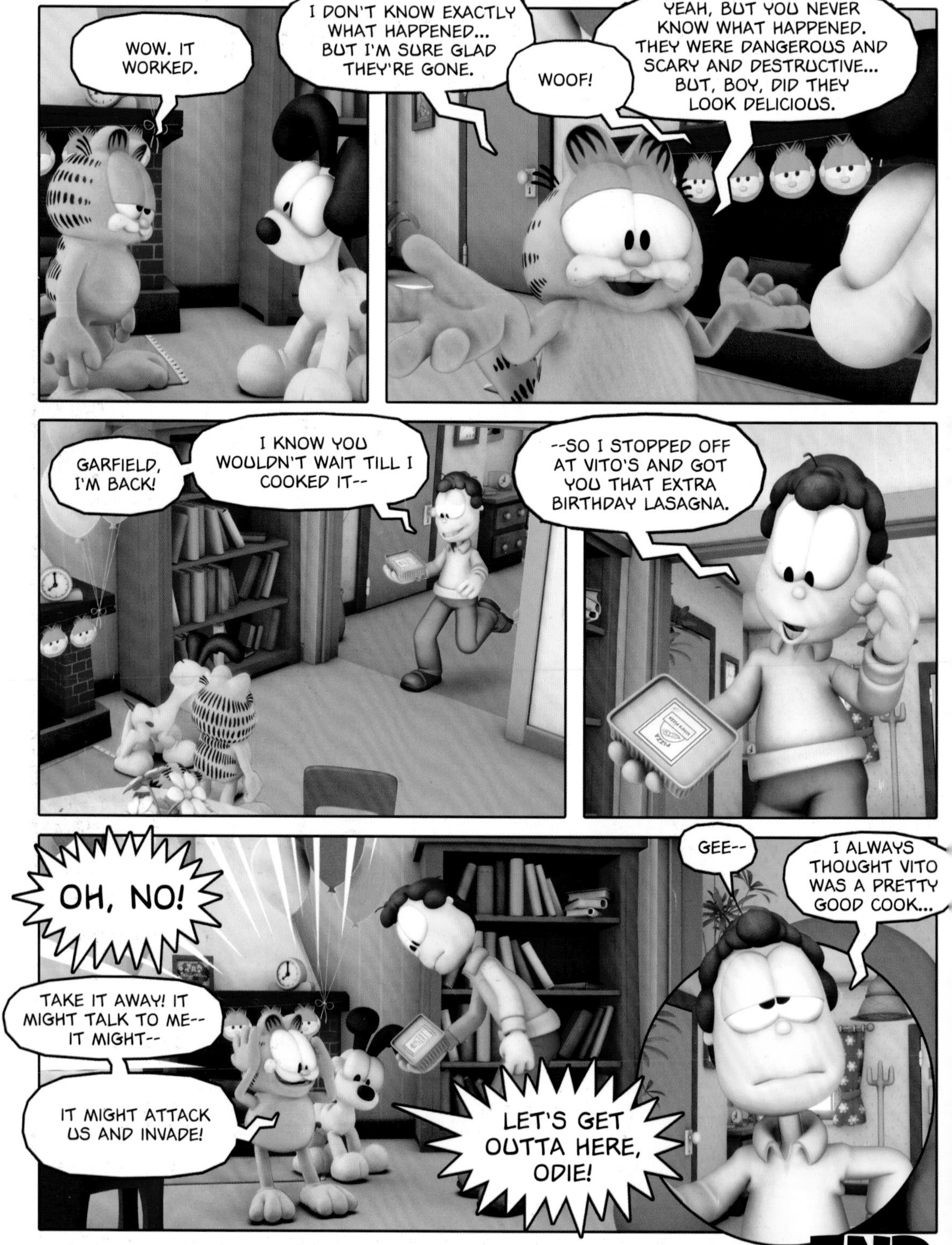
WOW. IT WORKED.
I DON'T KNOW EXACTLY WHAT HAPPENED... BUT I'M SURE GLAD THEY'RE GONE.
WOOF!
YEAH, BUT YOU NEVER KNOW WHAT HAPPENED. THEY WERE DANGEROUS AND SCARY AND DESTRUCTIVE... BUT, BOY, DID THEY LOOK DELICIOUS.
GARFIELD, I'M BACK!
I KNOW YOU WOULDN'T WAIT TILL I COOKED IT--
--SO I STOPPED OFF AT VITO'S AND GOT YOU THAT EXTRA BIRTHDAY LASAGNA.
OH, NO!
TAKE IT AWAY! IT MIGHT TALK TO ME-- IT MIGHT--
IT MIGHT ATTACK US AND INVADE!
LET'S GET OUTTA HERE, ODIE!
GEE--
I ALWAYS THOUGHT VITO WAS A PRETTY GOOD COOK...
END

WATCH OUT FOR PAPERCUTZ™

Welcome to the seriously-silly, space-invading, second THE GARFIELD SHOW graphic novel from Papercutz, those lasagna and cat-loving folks dedicated to publishing great graphic novels for all ages. I'm Jim Salicrup, the Editor-in-Chief and crazed comics collector here with a fun activity page just for you! While there aren't any mind-boggling cash prizes like on "Million Dollar Name That Fish," we hope that you'll enjoy our "Zero Dollar Name That Cat" quiz! It's really simple, just name the cartoon cats below and the Papercutz series that they appear in. Ready? Then let's begin…

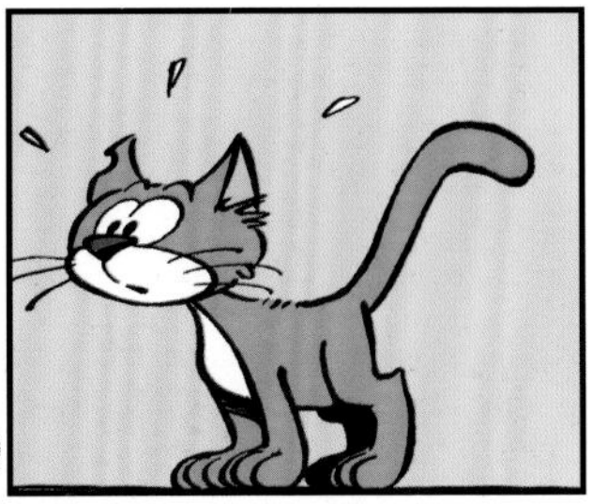

#1________________

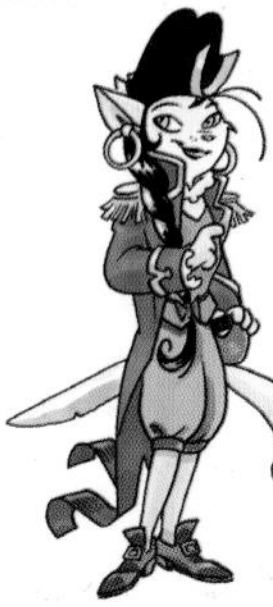

Geronimo Stilton © Atlantyca S.p.A.

#2________________

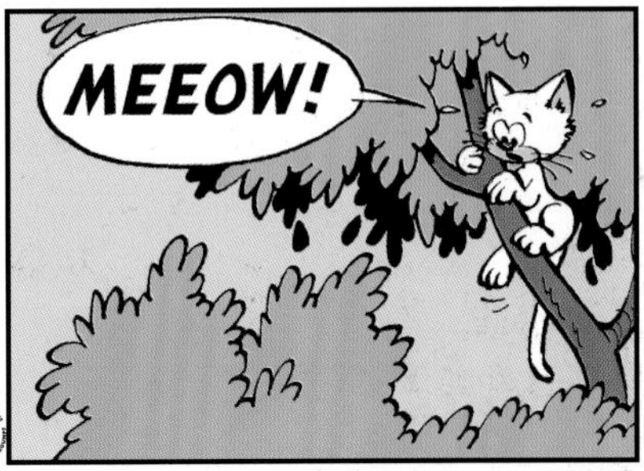
MEEOW!
© Peyo - 2013

#3________________

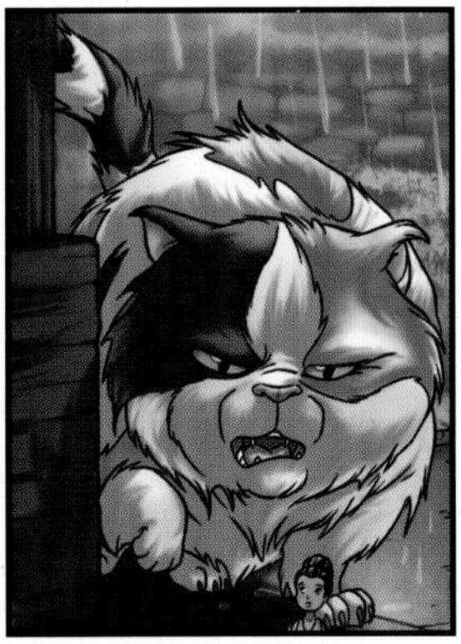

Disney Fairies © Disney Enterprises

#4________________

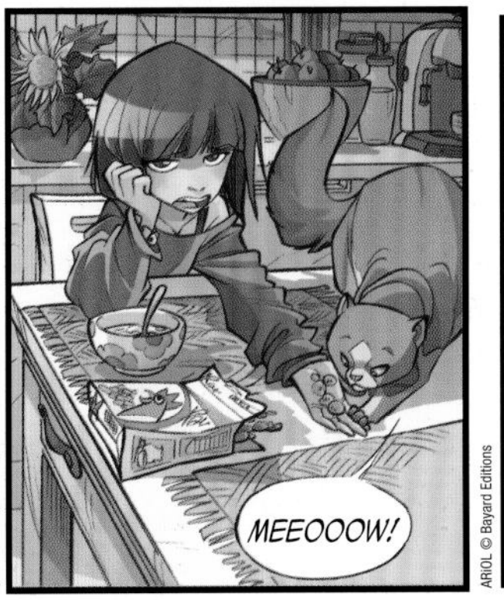
MEEOOOW!

Sybil the Backpack Fairy © Éditions du Lombard

#5________________

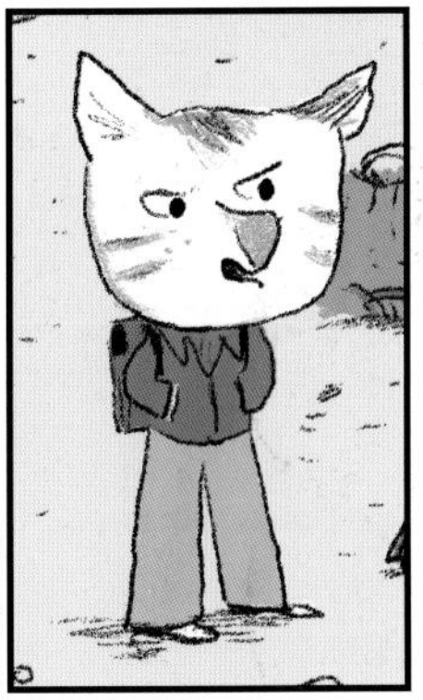

ARiOL © Bayard Editions

#6________________

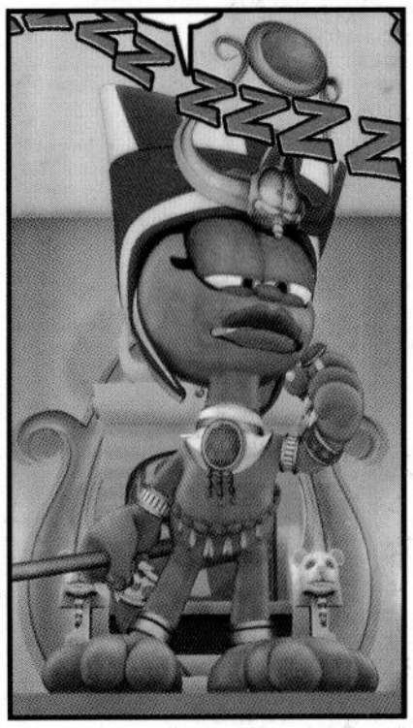

Garfield © PAWS, Inc.

#7________________

We warn you, one of the above is actually a trick question. For the answers just turn the page upside-down and read the tiny type below.

Finally, for all you longtime Garfield fans (isn't that just about everyone?), don't miss THE GARFIELD SHOW #3 "Long Lost Lyman," which answers one of the longest running mysteries in Garfield history!

Thanks,

Jim

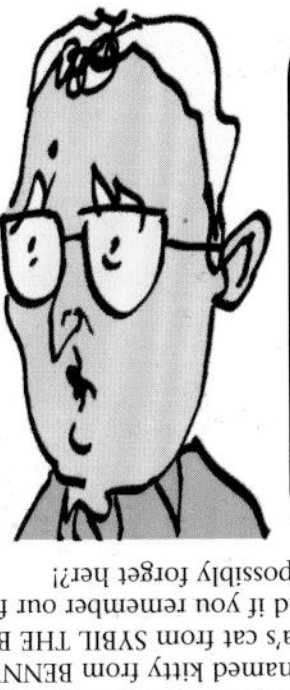

STAY IN TOUCH!

EMAIL:	SALICRUP@PAPERCUTZ.COM
WEB:	WWW.PAPERCUTZ.COM
TWITTER:	@PAPERCUTZGN
FACEBOOK:	PAPERCUTZGRAPHICNOVELS
BIRTHDAY CARDS:	PAPERCUTZ, 160 BROADWAY, SUITE 700, EAST WING, NEW YORK, NY 10038

ANSWERS: 1) That's Gargamel's only friend Azrael, from THE SMURFS, THE SMURFS CHRISTMAS, and THE SMURFS ANTHOLOGY. 2) Look out for Tersilla of Catatonia, the defacto leader of the Pirate Cats in GERONIMO STILTON. 3) Not the trick question—you can name this unnamed kitty from BENNY BREAKIRON #2. We call her "Voilà!" 4) That's Mr. Twitches from TINKER BELL AND THE GREAT FAIRY RESCUE, of course! 5) That's Macaroon, Nina's cat from SYBIL THE BACKPACK FAIRY. 6) Okay, this is the trick question! That's Timberwolf, and as his name would indicate, he's a timberwolf, not a cat, from ARiOL 7) And if you remember our first Garfield series, GARFIELD & Co, that's Neferkity, High Preistess of the Goddess Kat-Ra! How can you possibly forget her?!

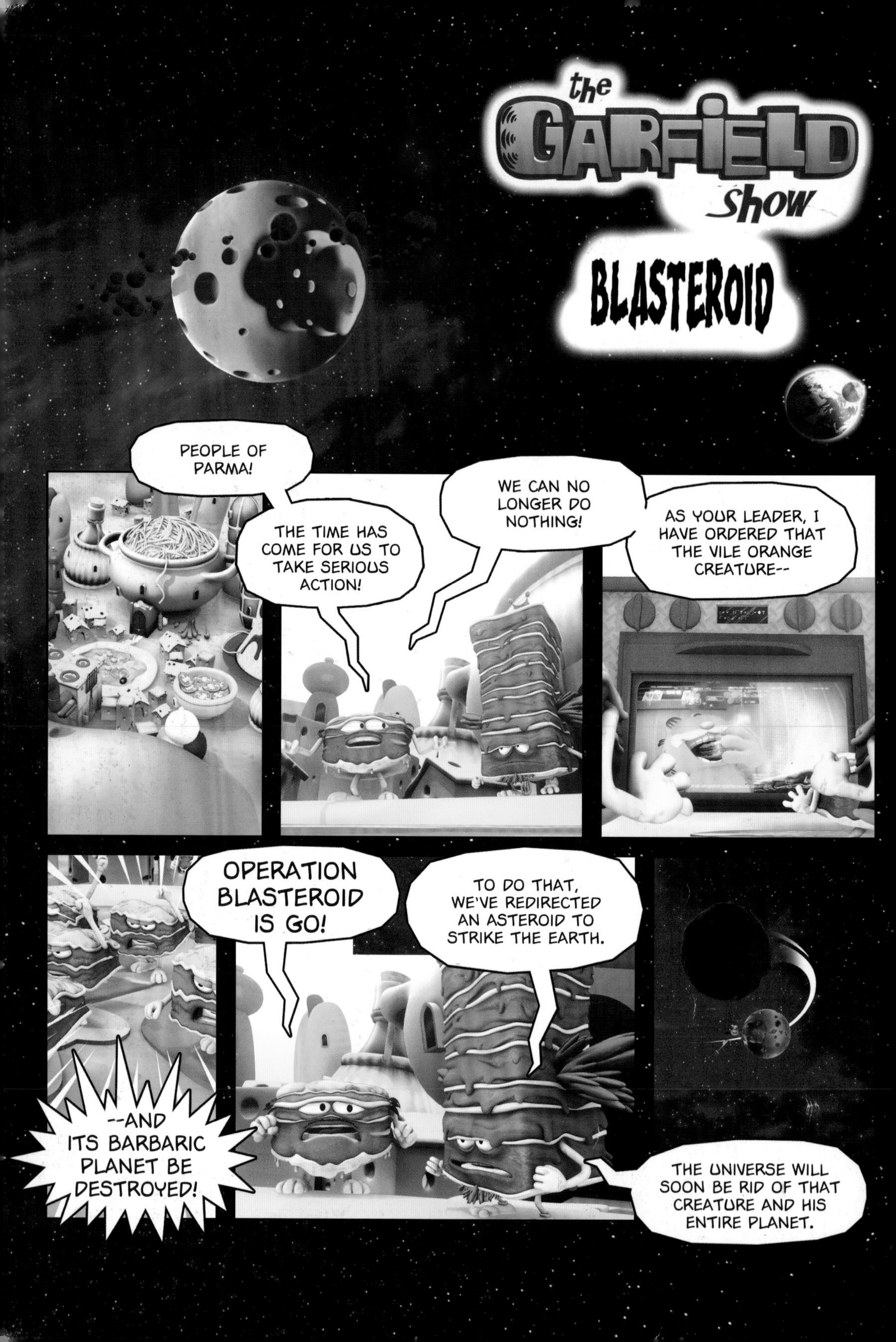
the GARFIELD show
BLASTEROID
PEOPLE OF PARMA!
THE TIME HAS COME FOR US TO TAKE SERIOUS ACTION!
WE CAN NO LONGER DO NOTHING!
AS YOUR LEADER, I HAVE ORDERED THAT THE VILE ORANGE CREATURE--
--AND ITS BARBARIC PLANET BE DESTROYED!
OPERATION BLASTEROID IS GO!
TO DO THAT, WE'VE REDIRECTED AN ASTEROID TO STRIKE THE EARTH.
THE UNIVERSE WILL SOON BE RID OF THAT CREATURE AND HIS ENTIRE PLANET.

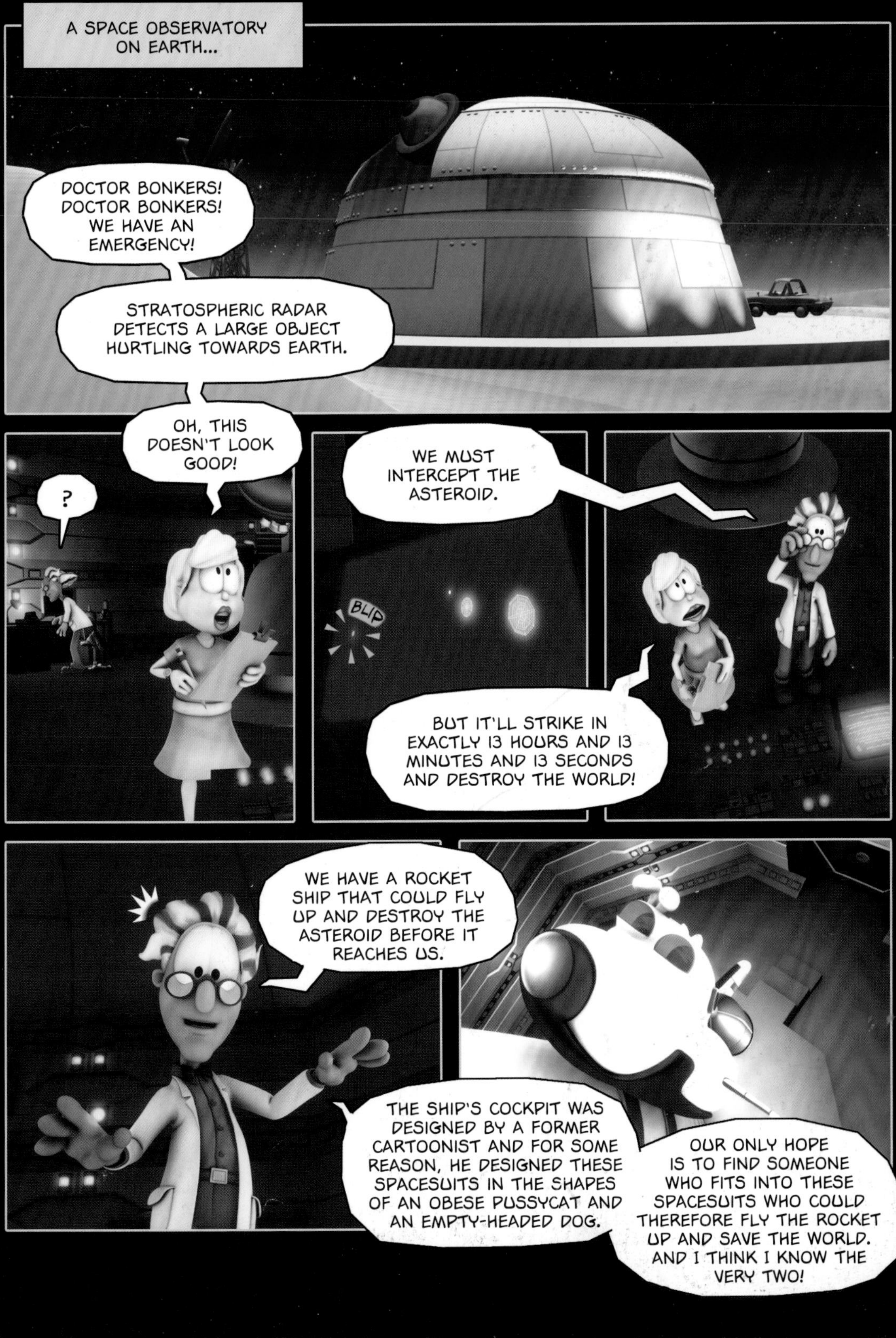
A SPACE OBSERVATORY ON EARTH...
DOCTOR BONKERS! DOCTOR BONKERS! WE HAVE AN EMERGENCY!
STRATOSPHERIC RADAR DETECTS A LARGE OBJECT HURTLING TOWARDS EARTH.
OH, THIS DOESN'T LOOK GOOD!
?
WE MUST INTERCEPT THE ASTEROID.
BLIP
BUT IT'LL STRIKE IN EXACTLY 13 HOURS AND 13 MINUTES AND 13 SECONDS AND DESTROY THE WORLD!
WE HAVE A ROCKET SHIP THAT COULD FLY UP AND DESTROY THE ASTEROID BEFORE IT REACHES US.
THE SHIP'S COCKPIT WAS DESIGNED BY A FORMER CARTOONIST AND FOR SOME REASON, HE DESIGNED THESE SPACESUITS IN THE SHAPES OF AN OBESE PUSSYCAT AND AN EMPTY-HEADED DOG.
OUR ONLY HOPE IS TO FIND SOMEONE WHO FITS INTO THESE SPACESUITS WHO COULD THEREFORE FLY THE ROCKET UP AND SAVE THE WORLD. AND I THINK I KNOW THE VERY TWO!

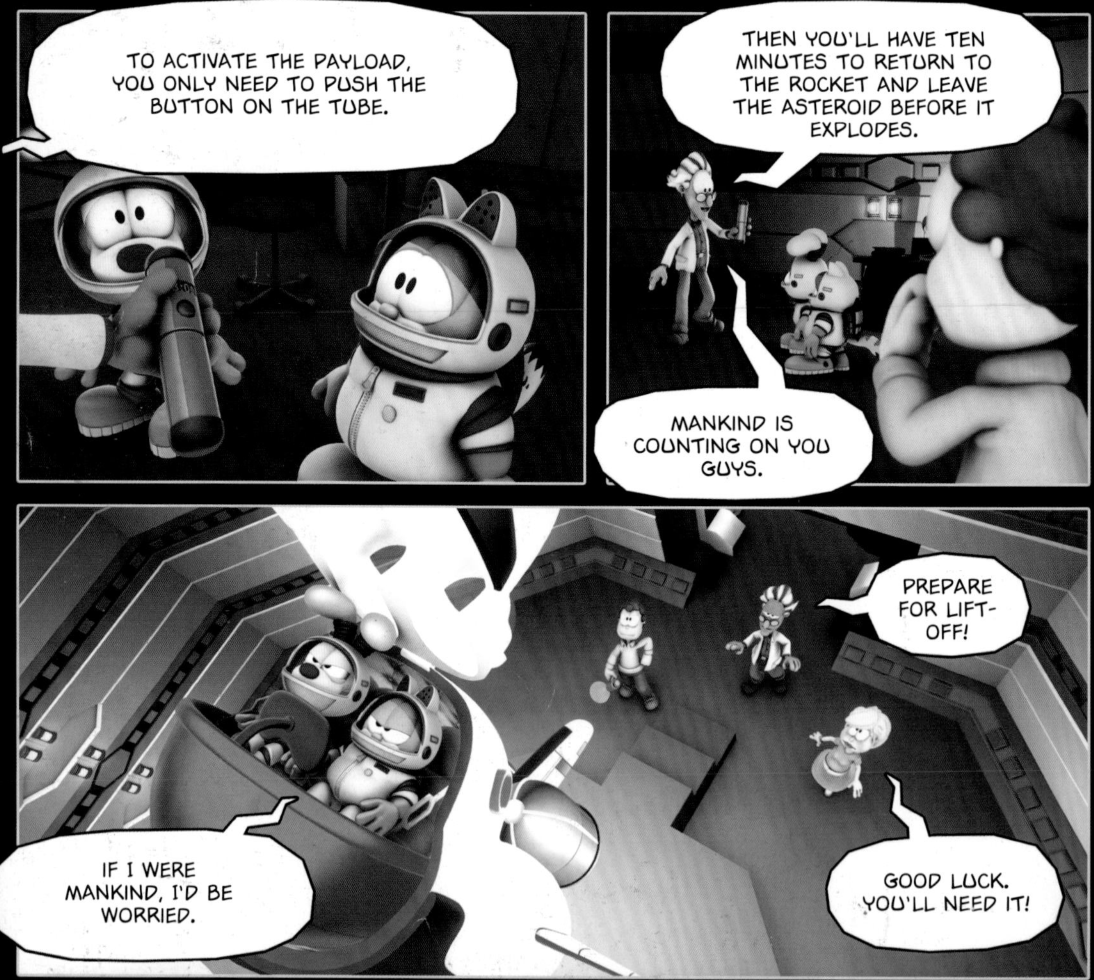
TO ACTIVATE THE PAYLOAD, YOU ONLY NEED TO PUSH THE BUTTON ON THE TUBE.
THEN YOU'LL HAVE TEN MINUTES TO RETURN TO THE ROCKET AND LEAVE THE ASTEROID BEFORE IT EXPLODES.
MANKIND IS COUNTING ON YOU GUYS.
PREPARE FOR LIFT-OFF!
IF I WERE MANKIND, I'D BE WORRIED.
GOOD LUCK. YOU'LL NEED IT!

LIFT-OFF IN T-MINUS 9 SECONDS.
8
7
4
3
2
1
BLAST OFF!
VROOOO
WHAT HAPPENED TO 6 AND 5?
NO TIME FOR 6 AND 5. YOU'VE GOT A WORLD TO SAVE!
⊰SNIF!⊱ ODIE... DO YOU SMELL SOMETHING FAMILIAR?
IF I DIDN'T KNOW BETTER, I'D SAY IT'S..
IT IS! BEEF... GARLIC... FINELY CHOPPED ONION...
YES! JUST AS I THOUGHT!
PLOP
THIS ASTEROID... IT'S A GIANT MEATBALL! WE'RE ON A MEAT-EOR!

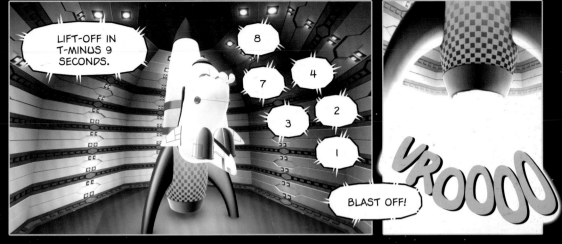

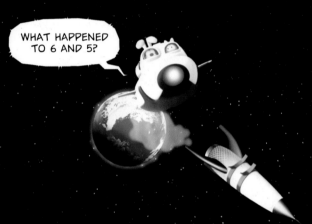

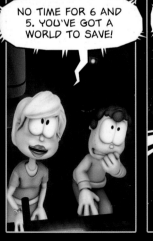

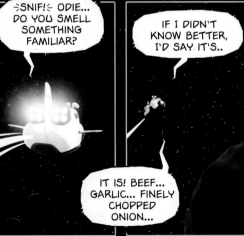

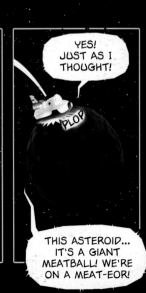

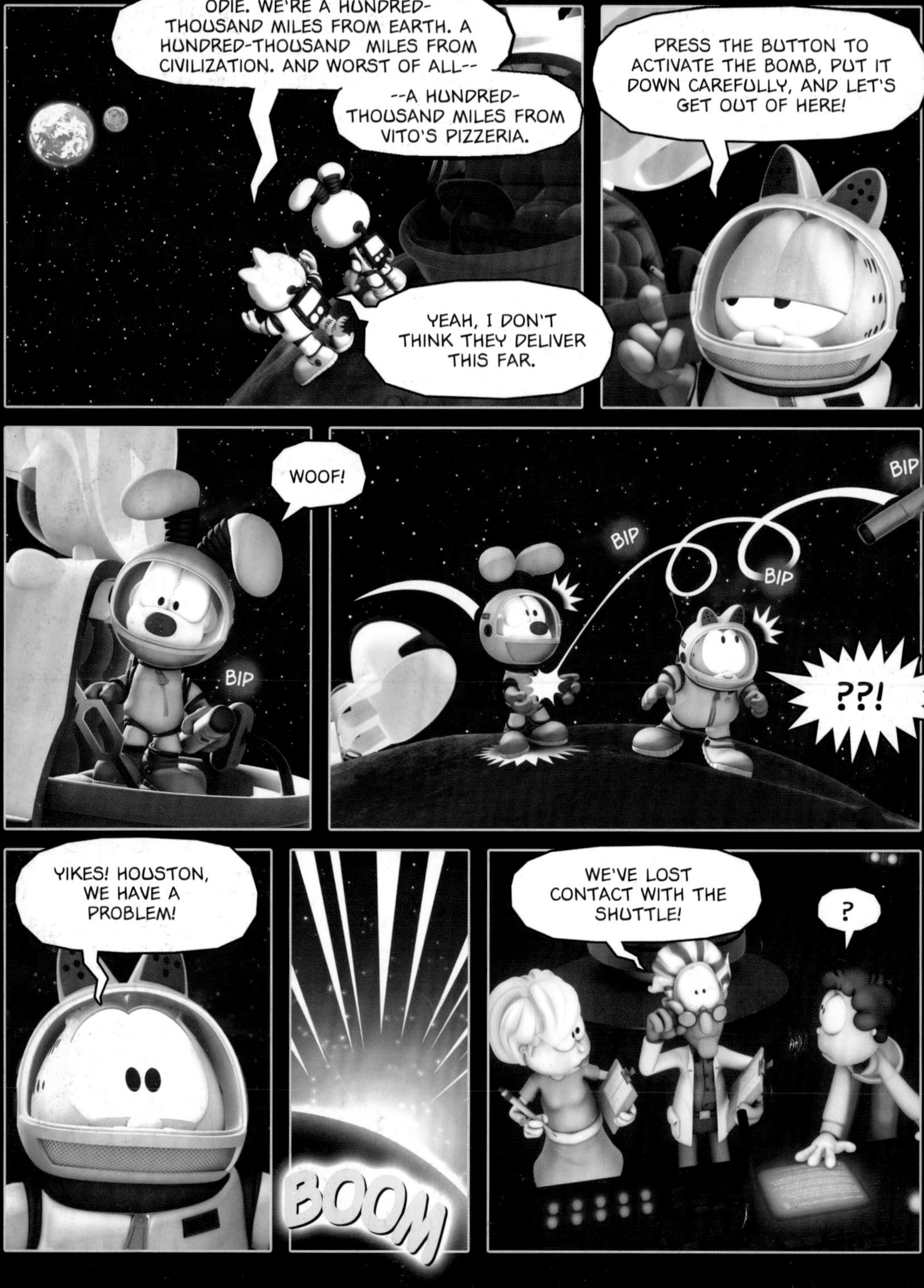
ODIE. WE'RE A HUNDRED-THOUSAND MILES FROM EARTH. A HUNDRED-THOUSAND MILES FROM CIVILIZATION. AND WORST OF ALL--
--A HUNDRED-THOUSAND MILES FROM VITO'S PIZZERIA.
YEAH, I DON'T THINK THEY DELIVER THIS FAR.
PRESS THE BUTTON TO ACTIVATE THE BOMB, PUT IT DOWN CAREFULLY, AND LET'S GET OUT OF HERE!
WOOF!
BIP
BIP
BIP
BIP
??!
YIKES! HOUSTON, WE HAVE A PROBLEM!
BOOM
WE'VE LOST CONTACT WITH THE SHUTTLE!
?

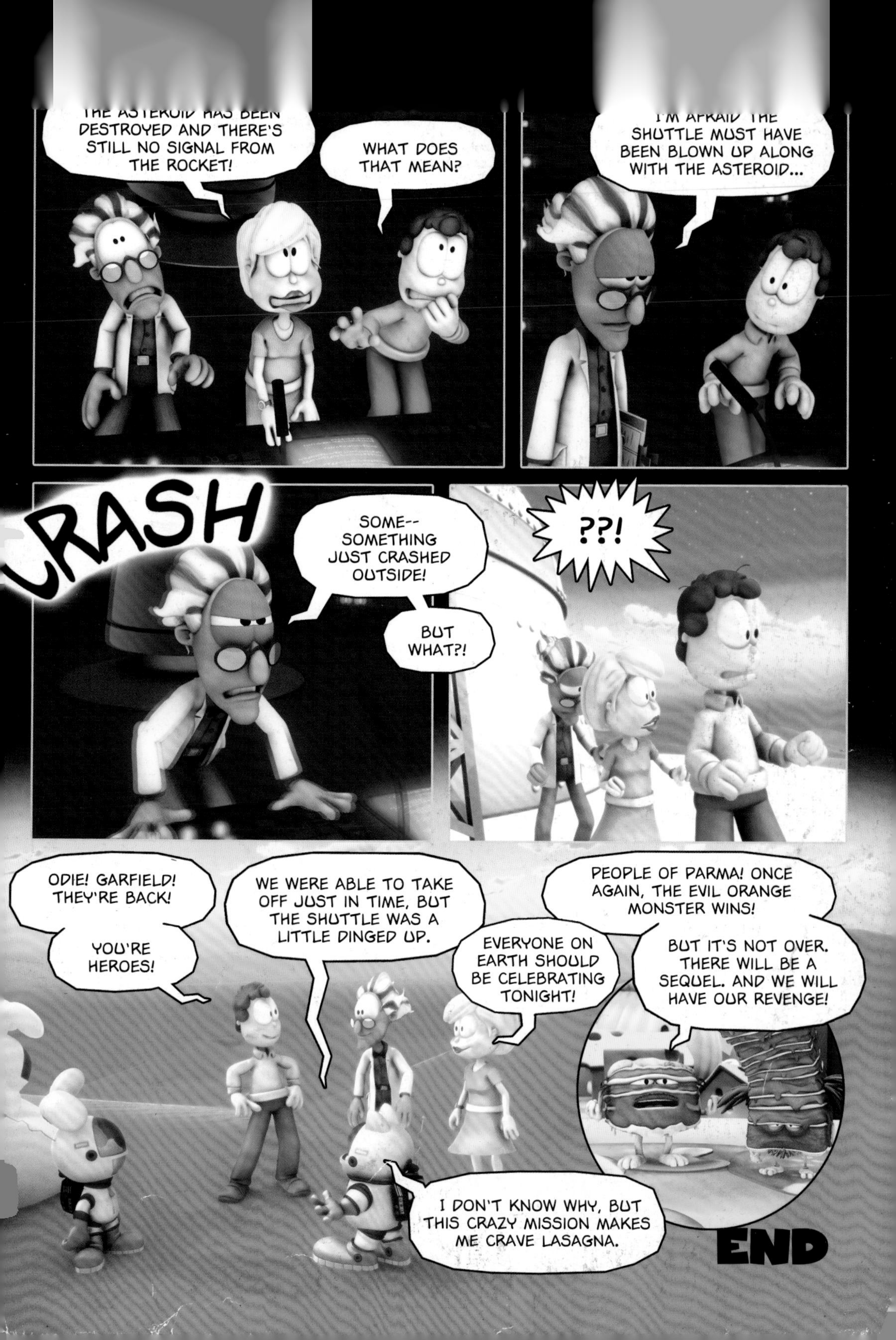
DESTROYED AND THERE'S STILL NO SIGNAL FROM THE ROCKET!
WHAT DOES THAT MEAN?
SHUTTLE MUST HAVE BEEN BLOWN UP ALONG WITH THE ASTEROID...
RASH
SOME-- SOMETHING JUST CRASHED OUTSIDE!
BUT WHAT?!
??!
ODIE! GARFIELD! THEY'RE BACK!
YOU'RE HEROES!
WE WERE ABLE TO TAKE OFF JUST IN TIME, BUT THE SHUTTLE WAS A LITTLE DINGED UP.
EVERYONE ON EARTH SHOULD BE CELEBRATING TONIGHT!
PEOPLE OF PARMA! ONCE AGAIN, THE EVIL ORANGE MONSTER WINS!
BUT IT'S NOT OVER. THERE WILL BE A SEQUEL. AND WE WILL HAVE OUR REVENGE!
I DON'T KNOW WHY, BUT THIS CRAZY MISSION MAKES ME CRAVE LASAGNA.
END

More Great Graphic Novels from PAPERCUTZ™

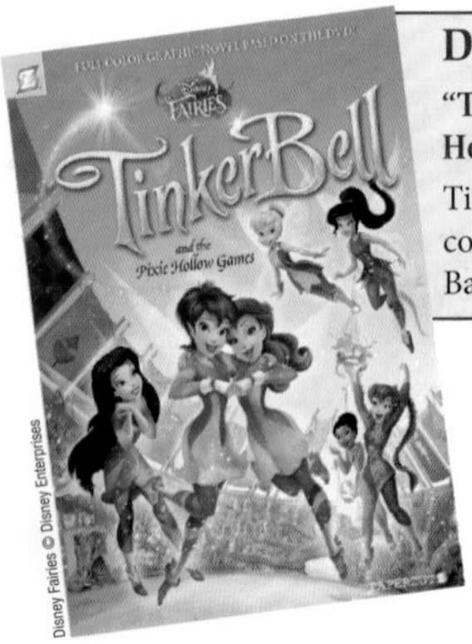
Disney Fairies
Tinker Bell
and the Pixie Hollow Games
PAPERCUTZ

DISNEY FAIRIES #13
"Tinker Bell and the Pixie Hollow Games"

Tink and her fairy friends gather to compete in the Pixie Hollow Games. Based on the hit TV special!

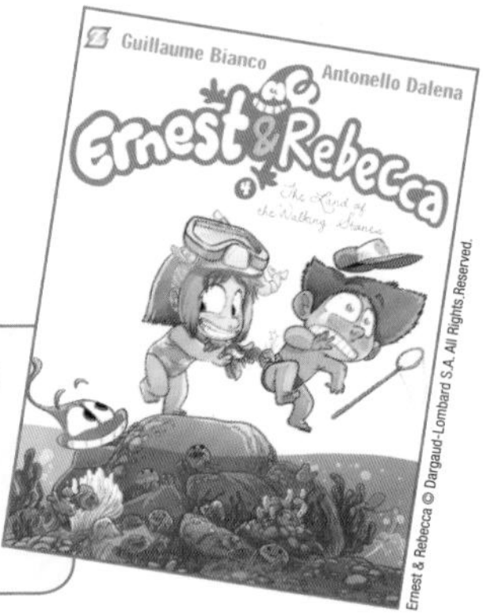
Guillaume Bianco
Antonello Dalena
Ernest & Rebecca
The Land of the Walking Stones

ERNEST & REBECCA #4
"The Land of Walking Stones"

A 6 ½ year old girl and her microbial buddy against the world!

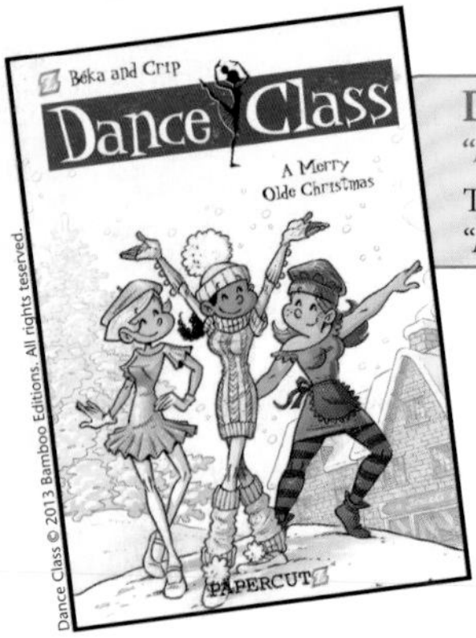
Béka and Crip
Dance Class
A Merry Olde Christmas
PAPERCUTZ

DANCE CLASS #6
"A Merry Olde Christmas"

The girls travel to Russia to perform "A Christmas Carol"!

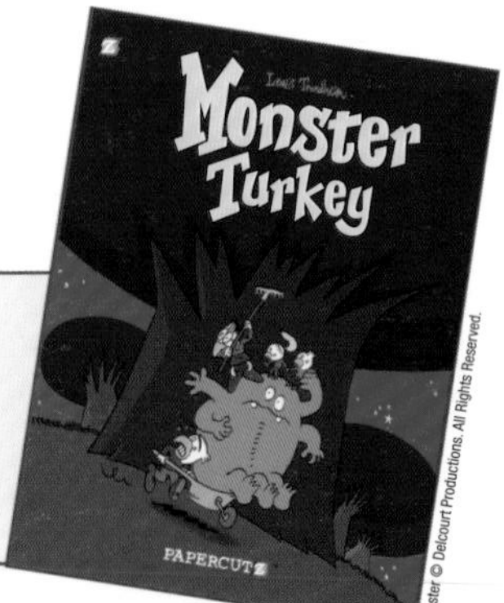
Monster
Turkey
PAPERCUTZ

MONSTER #4
"Monster Turkey"

The almost normal adventures of an almost ordinary family... with a pet monster!

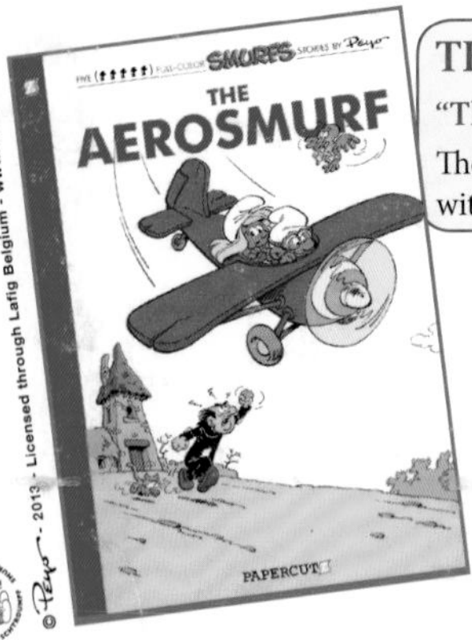
SMURFS
THE AEROSMURF
PAPERCUTZ

THE SMURFS #16
"The Aerosmurf"

The continuing adventures of the smurf with a dream... to fly!

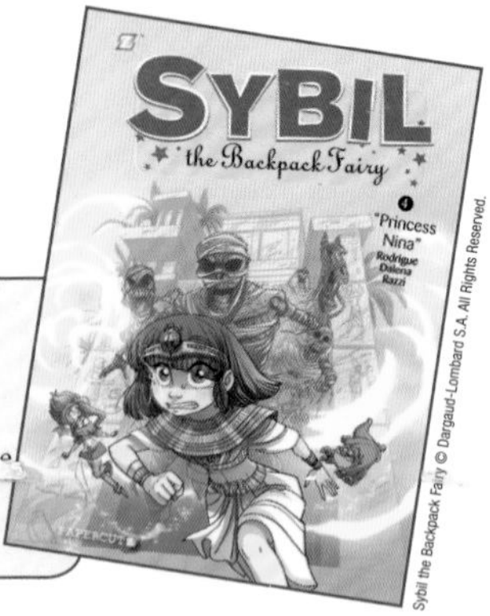
SYBIL
the Backpack Fairy
"Princess Nina"
PAPERCUTZ

SYBIL THE BACKPACK FAIRY #4
"Princess Nina"

Sybil and Nina's excellent adventure through time!

Available at better booksellers everywhere!

Or order directly from us! DISNEY FAIRIES is available in paperback for $7.99, in hardcover for $11.99; ERNEST & REBECCA is $11.99 in hardcover only; DANCE CLASS is available in hardcover only for $11.99; MONSTER is available in hardcover only for $9.99; THE SMURFS are available in paperback for $5.99, in hardcover for $10.99; and SYBIL THE BACKPACK FAIRY is available in hardcover only for $11.99.

Please add $4.00 for postage and handling for the first book, add $1.00 for each additional book.
Please make check payable to NBM Publishing. Send to: PAPERCUTZ,160 Broadway, Suite 700, East Wing, New York, NY 10038 (1-800-886-1223) or order online at papercutz.com